# *Whoa, baby.*

*Sam sniffed the fragrance again. It smelled wonderful. Like the air after a rain, like the breeze at the ocean, like the way she felt when she had Pres's arms around her as they watched the sunset on the beach. . . .*

Maybe I'm fooling myself, *Sam thought. She sniffed the test strip another time.*

I love it! It's perfect! *she thought with excitement. For the first time she felt truly enthusiastic about Emma and Carrie's perfume enterprise. . . .*

# Sunset Magic

## CHERIE BENNETT

Sunset™
Island

SPLASH™

A BERKLEY / SPLASH BOOK

SUNSET MAGIC is an original publication of The Berkley Publishing Group. This work has never appeared before in book form.

SUNSET MAGIC

A Berkley Book / published by arrangement with General Licensing Company, Inc.

PRINTING HISTORY
Berkley edition / July 1994

All rights reserved.
Copyright © 1994 by General Licensing Company, Inc.
Cover art copyright © 1994 by
General Licensing Company, Inc.
This book may not be reproduced in whole or in part,
by mimeograph or any other means, without permission.
For information address: General Licensing Company, Inc.,
24 West 25th Street, New York, New York 10010.

A GLC BOOK

*Splash* and *Sunset Island* are trademarks belonging to
General Licensing Company, Inc.

ISBN: 0-425-14290-6

BERKLEY®
Berkley Books are published by
The Berkley Publishing Group,
200 Madison Avenue, New York, New York 10016.
BERKLEY and the "B" design
are trademarks belonging to Berkley Publishing Corporation.

PRINTED IN THE UNITED STATES OF AMERICA

10  9  8  7  6  5  4  3  2

For Jeff, happy fourth anniversary!

# ONE

"Now, *that* is what I call totally decadent," Sam Bridges said to her two best friends, Carrie Alden and Emma Cresswell, as the three of them left the Portland Mall's multiplex movie theater.

"The movie?" Carrie asked, blinking her eyes to try to adjust to the early afternoon sunlight.

"Naah," Sam replied. "That guy with the blond hair who just drove by in the red Jag. The male lead was hot, though, huh? I wouldn't mind being stuck on a desert island with him!"

"Sam, you already have a boyfriend," Emma reminded her as they followed the paved walkway toward the mall's main

1

entrance. "Besides, you are all talk and no action."

"A girl can dream, can't she?" Sam replied loftily. "You should read this romance novel I read recently. It was all about this woman in the 1890s who—"

"Sam!" Emma interrupted. "We don't want to hear the plot to a romance novel!"

"Your loss," Sam said with a shrug. "I was going to tell you the secret to keeping a guy happy forever—which is what I learned from this book, but now you'll never know."

"The secret to keeping a guy happy?" Carrie echoed, making a face. "Who cares?"

"You do," Sam replied, "as long as the guy is Billy."

The three friends entered the mall, which was practically deserted. It was an absolutely gorgeous summer day, and apparently everyone was either at work or out enjoying the sunshine.

"I think he should be thinking about keeping Carrie happy," Emma said.

"True," Sam agreed, pushing some of her wild red curls off her face. They passed an ice cream parlor window that featured a poster of a banana split. "Yum. Does that look decadent, or what?"

"I can feel my thighs expanding just looking at it," Carrie said with a sigh.

"Decadence," Sam pontificated as she led Carrie and Emma through the mall, "is all of us getting the same day off for once, being at the mall precisely when the doors open at ten A.M., and going to a movie that starts before noontime!"

"I thought you'd say decadence was lying on the beach with Pres next to you, feeding you peeled grapes," Emma suggested as they walked along, occasionally stopping to look into a shop window.

"Well, that, too," Sam agreed. "I just love the word. It sounds so . . . so evil."

Sam stopped to look in the window of a clothing store. *These clothes are seriously tacky,* she thought, grimacing as she eyed one particularly hideous green-and-white striped drop-waist number. *Who'd actually wear that?*

"Hey, my mom owns a dress almost exactly like that," Carrie said, pointing to the green-and-white horror.

*Oops,* Sam thought. *I'm glad I didn't insult it out loud.*

"Where are you leading us?" Carrie asked as Sam strode onward.

"The food court, where else?" Sam responded. "I'm starved."

"But we had a big breakfast right before the movie," Emma reminded her.

"So?" Sam asked. "That was two hours ago. Besides, didn't just *looking* at the picture of that giant banana split make you salivate?"

"Medical science should study you," Carrie joked. "You can be made to drool on cue."

"Speaking of drooling, check out that guy!" Sam whispered, staring at a brown-haired guy sitting on a bench, reading a magazine.

"What is it with you?" Carrie asked, laughing, "a cute guy is in the vicinity and your radar goes off or something?"

"I look but do not touch," Sam said solemnly. "I have turned over a new leaf. I am now a one-man woman."

They walked past the guy and Sam

turned around and walked backward, looking wistfully back at him.

"Down, girl," Carrie told Sam, pulling her back around.

They turned the corner and came to the food court, which featured seven or eight different kinds of takeout counters and restaurants, along with some tables in the middle.

"Let's meet back at the tables," Sam suggested.

Sam headed for a pizza stand, Carrie to a shop that sold ready-made salads, and Emma to a Japanese takeout restaurant.

"What's that?" Sam asked Emma suspiciously, eyeing Emma's tray when they'd all settled at a table.

"Sushi," Emma replied. "Try a piece."

"What's in it?" Sam asked warily.

"Oh, just be brave and take a bite," Emma coaxed.

Sam reached for one of the seaweed-wrapped circles and bit into it. She chewed for a moment. "Huh. Not bad." She took another bite. "It's actually pretty good."

"I never knew you had a taste for

seaweed and raw fish," Emma said casually.

"Yuck!" Sam gagged, spewing out the offending bite into her napkin.

"You should see the look on your face!" Carrie cried, hooting with laughter.

"Oh, very amusing," Sam replied.

*One thing about being with Emma and Carrie,* she thought, *life's always an adventure!*

As Sam ate her pizza and Emma and Carrie got off on a conversation about Carrie's photography, Sam's mind began to wander. She thought back on the circumstances that had brought her together with Emma and Carrie.

Sam couldn't even remember why she'd decided two summers ago that it would be fun to be an au pair for a summer, to live with a strange family and take care of their kids. *Oh, yeah, anything to get away from dreary small-town life,* she reminded herself. During her senior year of high school she'd traveled to New York from her tiny hometown of Junction, Kansas, for the International Au Pair Convention.

So had Emma and Carrie. And the three of them met there and immediately liked one another.

They were as different from one another as they could be. Sam was basically a country girl from a modest background (*though God knows I was not meant to stay that way,* Sam thought to herself) who was blessed with a talent for dancing and a great sense of style. The older of two daughters, the adopted child of a high school football coach and a mother who worked in a pharmacy, she wanted nothing more than to become rich and famous, and not necessarily in that order. She'd tried college—she'd had a dance scholarship to Kansas State—but had quit after less than a semester to be a dancer at Disney World.

*Not that my career lasted long there,* Sam recalled. *I got fired because my dancing was too original! The story of my life. The world just doesn't appreciate the unique!*

Carrie, on the other hand, came from an upper-middle-class home in suburban New Jersey, where her parents were both pediatricians. Her dream was to become a photojournalist after three more years at Yale.

Emma was a different story altogether. One of the Boston Cresswells, she came from one of the richest families in America. She didn't have to work a day in her life if she didn't want to. And yet Emma, who spoke five languages and had been educated at boarding school in Switzerland, had decided to work as an au pair anyway, and now wanted more than anything else to join the Peace Corps and go to Africa!

*Pretty different,* Sam thought. *We even look totally different. I'm tall and slender and have all this wild red hair, Carrie's a curvy brunette—she thinks too curvy, but I'd kill for her hooters, and Emma, well, Emma looks like you'd think Emma Cresswell would look, with perfect blond hair, perfect features, perfect everything!*

*And we're best friends. Lucky to be best friends. Lucky to have found jobs at the same location. And to be back on fabulous Sunset Island, this incredible resort island off the coast of Maine, working as au pairs for the second summer in a row! Life is strange sometimes. Very strange.*

She looked over at Carrie and Emma, who were still deep in conversation. *They are the best friends anybody ever had,* Sam thought. *Even if sometimes I do feel like I'm not nearly as smart as they are, or—*

"Do you want me to save you the last piece of sushi?" Emma asked Sam innocently.

Sam was pulled out of her reverie. "Gee, no thanks, Em," she replied. "Not unless you want me to hurl on the table." Sam ate the last two bites of her pizza. "Hey, did I mention how cute that top is?" she asked Carrie.

Carrie had on a short-sleeve navy blue crocheted sweater that flared and fell to her hips.

"Thanks," Carrie said. "My mom sent it to me. She said it was an 'I was thinking of you and I miss you' present."

*Wow,* Sam marveled. *The same woman who would wear that hideous green-and-white garmento picked out that cute sweater.*

9

"Mom said her best friend, Patrice, picked it out," Carrie continued. "I love my mother, but she's pretty hopeless when it comes to fashion."

*No kidding.* Sam slurped up the last of her Coke. "Well, all I have to say is that sweater is cuter than anything we saw today in the mall."

Before the movie, the girls had wandered through at least a half dozen stores. Sam hadn't been impressed with any of them. In fact, in her opinion all three of them were dressed better than any of the mannequins in the store windows. For example, with Carrie's crocheted top she had on navy blue leggings and high-top sneakers. Emma, immaculate as always, had on a white lace baby-doll top with shorts, and little white flats. Sam looked down at her own outfit—oversize jeans held up with black velvet suspenders, to which she had attached various rhinestone baubles she had found and glued to safety pins. Under the suspenders she had on a tie-dyed baby-style T-shirt covered with red peace symbols. On her feet were her trademark red cowboy boots.

"I mean, tell me the truth," Sam said. "Did you see one thing that was unique and fabulous that you had to have?"

"That embroidered velvet vest was beautiful," Carrie said wistfully. "But I couldn't afford it without robbing a bank."

"See, that's my point," Sam insisted. "You saw only one thing you liked, and it cost a mint. I mean, I could make a vest like that with a velvet remnant and some lace and ribbons in about two hours."

"The three of us have really different taste," Emma pointed out. "We'd probably never agree on clothing, anyway."

"At least you don't live in designer originals anymore like you used to," Sam said. "That's progress."

Emma smiled. "Only the very best," she teased at her own expense. "Clean lines, understated elegance—"

"With prices that could feed a small island nation," Sam added. She patted her stomach. "I'm trying to decide if I'm still hungry."

"In my next life I'm coming back with your metabolism," Carrie told Sam.

"Here's what kills me," Sam said, back

on her train of thought. "Someone decides a new look is supposed to be hot— like . . . like midi skirts. Remember them? They weren't short and they weren't long. They looked equally awful on everyone. But were the stores full of these uggo things? Yes, they were."

"I bet you never wore one," Carrie said.

"I'd rather go out naked," Sam decreed. "I'm telling you, the monsters have more style and originality than these design-ers!"

The "monsters" were Becky and Allie Jacobs, the precocious fourteen-year-old twins who she took care of. The Jacobs twins had recently gotten jobs as counselors-in-training at Club Sunset Island, the day camp on the island, so Sam was finding herself with a lot more free time during the day.

"Actually, this summer the twins have been dressing really cute," Carrie said. "I remember when you took care of them last summer and they wore too much makeup, with their clothes too tight—"

"Meaning that I have been a good

influence on them," Sam translated. "Gee, Mr. Jacobs ought to give me a raise."

"So, do you still want to go throw eggs at the window of Sweethearts?" Carrie asked.

Sweethearts was the second store they had visited in the mall. It was full of some of the worst clothes that Sam had ever seen—everything was super-conservative, boring, and out of date.

Sam shuddered as she recalled the horror in the window at Sweethearts—a pale pink dress with a white lace collar and little white hearts marching across the bodice, bell sleeves, and a huge pink sash. And the price tag had been in the three digits. "They're not worth a prison sentence," Sam decided. "But someone should call the fashion police on them. Hey, you want that last tomato?" She pointed to a lone tomato that Carrie had left uneaten.

Carrie shook her head no. Instantly, Sam picked it up and popped it in her mouth.

"It'd never replace pizza," she commented, "but I believe in eating veggies

13

once a year, whether I need to or not." She reached for Emma's iced tea and took a sip. "Anyway," Sam continued, "I could make better clothes than they sell in there. I guarantee it."

"You think?" Carrie asked.

"I know!"

"But didn't you once tell me that you can't sew?" Emma said. "I remember you said you almost flunked home ec for putting the panel of an A-line skirt in sideways."

"So?" Sam pulled on her suspenders. "I made these—no sewing involved. You can do incredible things with safety pins, actually."

"Without looking like a reject from a punk rock band?" Carrie wondered.

Sam gave her a withering look. "Carrie Alden, have I ever in my life looked like a reject from anything?"

"Good point," Carrie replied with a laugh. "I guess this makes you the only girl in 4-H who never learned to sew."

"But she did have a pet pig!" Emma reminded Carrie. This was a fact they had found out from Sam's parents when

14

they'd seen them in New York City earlier that summer. Carrie and Emma still couldn't get over it.

"Hey, do not rag on my porker," Sam warned. "Cookie was the coolest. He was *some pig*! At least I was in 4-H, unlike you two uncouth creatures."

"I have to admit you're right," Carrie said. "4-H isn't real big in Teaneck, New Jersey."

"Or at Aubergame Academy in Switzerland," Emma added.

"See, I have known exotic worlds about which the two of you have only dreamed," Sam decreed. She eyed a donut shop across the food court. "Anyone want to join me for sugar shock?"

The three girls headed over to the donut shop, where Sam bought herself two jelly donuts, which she proceeded to devour. "Seriously delish," she said between bites, licking powdered sugar off her fingers.

"Let's walk by Macy's, okay?" Emma asked. "I want to look at their perfume display."

15

"Thinking about Sunset Magic, huh?" Sam asked, polishing off the first donut.

"A little," Emma replied.

"A lot," Carrie said. "At least I am."

As they walked through the mall toward Macy's, Sam only half listened as Carrie and Emma compared notes about Sunset Magic, the new fragrance that they were involved in creating.

The whole thing seemed to Sam to be just a little unreal. Only a short while earlier in the summer, Emma and Sam had met Erin Kane, who had been picked to be the new backup singer for the band Flirting With Danger, for which Emma and Sam sang backup. All three girls had liked Erin immediately—Emma especially, and they had all become fast friends.

It turned out that Erin's father had been involved in the perfume business as a "nose"—the guy who actually creates new fragrances. But he'd lost his job in a cost-cutting measure. One night, when all the girls were over at Erin's house for a barbecue, they'd come up with the idea of creating a perfume of their own, with Erin's father's help.

*Now,* Sam thought as they made their way over to the perfume-testing section of Macy's department store, *with Emma's money financing the project and Carrie's brains for business, they're actually doing it!*

She looked at Emma and Carrie out of the corner of her eye. *I hope Emma isn't getting into this just to help her forget Kurt,* Sam thought. *A perfume can not replace the lost love of your life.*

Sam checked her Mickey Mouse watch. "We better book," she told her friends. "We have to be at Super Shots in fifteen minutes."

Just for fun, the girls had made appointments together at Super Shots, a glamour-photography studio in the mall. For a special offer of only thirty dollars each, they would get their makeup and hair done by a professional makeup artist, as well as the use of the props, accessories, and costumes that were available in the studio. Then a photographer would pose them and take a bunch of shots. They'd have to pay for any blowups of the shots they might want, but they figured that if they hated the photos they'd be out only thirty dollars, and they'd still have a lot of fun.

"The perfume's down there," Emma said, pointing past the cosmetics counter.

"What do you think of this one, Sam?" Emma asked a moment later as she picked up a bottle of something called Lost Horizons and sprayed it on Sam's arm.

Sam cautiously lifted her bare arm and took a sniff.

"Barf me," she commented. "It smells like cough syrup. Only worse."

Carrie picked up another bottle. It featured silhouettes of a couple kissing on its side. She sniffed the perfume. "Ugh. Too strong and flowery. It smells like something my history teacher used to wear in high school—it always made me sick."

"Sunset Magic will be so much better!" Emma said, her eyes shining.

"I think you've got a real problem with it," Sam said flatly.

Emma looked at her. "What?"

"The name."

18

"You don't like it?" Carrie asked.

"I've been telling you and telling you," Sam said. "A perfume needs an identity."

"And?" Emma asked.

"And . . ." Sam echoed, "*I* am an identity. It should be called Sam!"

"Gee, where have I heard that before?" Carrie teased.

"From me," Sam admitted, spraying a perfume on her wrist and taking a sniff. "Look at it this way. Elizabeth Taylor has her own perfume. Now, what has she got that I haven't got?"

"Money and fame?" Carrie guessed.

"Exactly!" Sam replied triumphantly. "She doesn't need a perfume named after her. I do!"

# TWO

"Midnight picnic on the beach, yes!" Sam declared as she strode into the plush client waiting area at Super Shots. Emma and Carrie were sitting on a floral print couch, their heads close together, deep in a murmured conversation.

"Yo, fellow foxes, wait till you hear what Pres and I are doing tonight!" Sam said eagerly.

Carrie and Emma paid no attention to her.

"Hel-lo!" Sam called.

"What?" Carrie asked distractedly, finally looking over at Sam.

Sam sat in the stuffed chair opposite them, feeling slightly miffed because her friends seemed so distracted. "I just called

Pres to find out about what we're doing tonight."

"Oh" was all Emma said.

"You're supposed to inquire as to what exciting activity we might have cooked up," Sam explained dryly.

"We were talking about something completely different," Carrie explained.

"Why do I have a feeling it starts with a *p* and ends with an *e* and has something to do with your nose?" Sam asked.

"You're right," Emma agreed, still sounding distracted. She turned back to Carrie. "I agree about the marketing aspect of things," she said. "We need to itemize the budget carefully, and then figure out just how word of mouth will play into things."

Sam made a noise of disgust under her breath. "So," she said loudly, "what time are they actually taking us in for our pictures?"

"Soon, I guess," Emma replied diffidently. She then turned her attention back to Carrie, and within seconds the two of them were back in their conversation, totally engrossed.

*Well, that's pretty rude,* Sam thought to herself.

"Uh, excuse me future empire-builders," Sam said. "But I thought we were supposed to be *three* friends on a day off together, remember?"

Carrie and Emma both looked up at Sam at the same time, and the same sheepish look crossed their faces.

"Sorry," Carrie mumbled.

"You're right." Emma nodded agreement.

"We just got a little caught up in what we were talking about," Emma explained.

"What a shocker," Sam said dryly. "Don't you ever get tired of talking about perfume?" Sam asked, reaching over and picking up a fashion magazine that was on one of the tables in the waiting area and flipping through the pages.

"No," Emma said, "not really."

"It's not the perfume so much as it is the idea that it's our own business," Carrie explained.

"Your own business," Sam commented. "Meanwhile, there are so many other interesting things to talk about."

"Like what?" Carrie asked.

"Jeez, you slay me!" Sam cried, throwing down the magazine. "You're turning into your parents! Guys, for example. Love. Lust. More guys."

"It's just that we're getting the final perfume samples in from Erin's dad in a couple of days," Emma explained. "And we're going to have to pick one for Sunset Magic."

"And then set up our marketing plan," Carrie added.

"And then get it on the market," Emma said.

"And monitor sales—"

"And restock—"

"And take care of all the paperwork, and taxes, toc," Carrie concluded.

*Gee, it sounds like a ton of laughs,* Sam thought to herself. *My two best friends are playing Junior Achievement when they should be having fun.*

"You know," Carrie said, taking a sip from the glass of iced tea the receptionist had given them, "we'd be happy to have you get more involved."

"Yes!" Emma said enthusiastically.

"You're so creative and you have so many great ideas."

"I'll pass," Sam replied. "I intended for this summer to be fun."

"But this is fun!" Emma replied.

Sam rolled her eyes, then she leaned closer to Emma. "Are you sure that you're not getting all involved in this because of . . . you-know-who?"

Emma looked confused.

"I mean Kurt," Sam filled in. "You know, so you'll be so busy that you won't have to think about him."

"I guess that could be part of it," Emma admitted. She looked over at Carrie. "But it's more than that, too. You know, my dad was born poor. Then he married my mother, who was always rich. And Daddy decided he had to prove to everyone that he could make his own fortune. And he did."

"So you're saying that you are your father's daughter," Carrie said.

Emma nodded. "Exactly."

"Well, I hate to be the one to point this out to you," Sam intoned, "but if you weren't already rich, you wouldn't have

25

the capital to start this little business venture in the first place."

"We could have borrowed it from a bank, maybe," Carrie said.

"No, Sam's right," Emma admitted. "No bank would lend capital to nineteen-year-olds for their own fragrance business."

"I wasn't criticizing you—" Sam began.

"It's okay," Emma said, pushing some hair behind one ear. "But I still think—"

Just then the receptionist, an attractive young woman in a black minidress, called out to the girls, "Who's first?"

"Me!" Sam said, jumping to her feet. They'd already decided that Sam would go first, and then Carrie, and then Emma. Sam grabbed her dance bag, which contained some clothes and accessories, and headed for the back area of the studio.

"Just follow the green line on the floor," the receptionist told her. Sam looked down. Sure enough, there was a long green line with arrows next to it right at her feet.

"Go get 'em," Carrie encouraged her.

*Sure,* Sam was tempted to say, *you're*

*happy that I'm going first, so that you and Emma can keep talking about that dumb perfume business.* But Sam knew, deep down, that her friends were just excited about their venture, and so she kept her mouth shut.

She followed the green line on the floor until it turned right, leading into a door that said MAKEUP/DRESSING ROOM on it. The door was shut. Sam stood there for an instant, and then knocked.

"Come in!" said a husky female voice. Sam opened the door and stepped inside. Standing there by a gigantic vanity with all sorts of makeup on it was a tall, young blond woman in her twenties with an absolute ton of moussed-up hair. She looked at Sam curiously for a moment, and then a broad grin crossed her face.

"I know you," she said to Sam, "don't I?"

Sam racked her brain for a moment.

*She does look familiar,* Sam thought, *but I swear I can't place her.*

"Could be," Sam answered. "I'm Sam Bridges. You're . . ."

"Belinda," the young woman replied, a huge grin on her face.

"You're kidding," Sam said. "Is it really you?"

"It's me," Belinda assured her. "Say cheese, babe!" Then they both cracked up. The previous summer Belinda had been the makeup artist for photographer Flash Hathaway, who had conned Sam into posing for some lurid pictures. Belinda had actually been Flash's girl-friend sometime earlier, but at the time Sam had met her, she was his extremely sullen assistant.

Sam hugged Belinda. "I can't believe it! You look so different!"

"I let my hair go back to its natural color," Belinda explained. "I put on ten pounds. And I got happier!"

"You look great!" Sam replied. "But I thought you went back to Michigan after you quit Flash!" Sam said, walking to-ward the makeup chair that Belinda had offered her.

"I did," Belinda answered, taking a close look at Sam's face. "And then I went to the San Francisco Art Institute last year."

"So what are you doing back here again?" Sam asked, still surprised to see Belinda.

"Working," Belinda said. "I always loved Sunset Island. When a friend told me this place was opening up, I jumped at the chance to work in the area. Anyway, Flash isn't around, and he's the one I had to get away from." Belinda carefully began to blend some base into Sam's skin with a sponge.

"Emma saw him a while ago at a photo shoot," Sam told Belinda. "She said he was as noxious as ever."

"Ah, yes," Belinda agreed. "The human cesspool of the photographic world." She patted concealer a shade lighter than Sam's base under Sam's eyes, then carefully blended it in with a new sponge.

"I'm so glad to see you," Sam said, smiling at Belinda's reflection in the mirror.

"Same here," Belinda agreed. "Now, hold still while I transform you from merely fabulous into a ravishing beauty."

First Belinda lightly feathered in Sam's eyebrows with a reddish-brown pencil. Then she dusted Sam's eyelids with a neutral beige powder. Next she lined Sam's eyes, top and bottom with a brown pencil, smudging the line into her lash line. Plum and rust eye shadow went into the crease, carefully blended for a subtle look. Then Belinda stroked two coats of black mascara over Sam's lashes. Finally she dusted Sam's face with a loose neutral powder, then brushed some blush on the apple of Sam's cheeks.

"There," Belinda said, turning Sam's chair to face the mirror. "How do you like it?"

"It's terrif," Sam exclaimed, turning her head at different angles and admiring what she saw. "It's subtle, you know? You're really wonderful."

"True, true," Belinda agreed with a laugh. "Now, when you want that 'hot momma' look—like if you're planning on posing in some trashy lingerie or something, I'll deepen your lipstick and eye shadow."

"Please," Sam said, "don't remind me of trashy lingerie."

"Okay," Belinda said with a laugh. "So, what do you have in mind for your photos? I'm doubling as your stylist."

Sam had planned her shots in advance. She wanted to have a few taken in a new swimsuit she'd purchased at the Cheap Boutique a couple of days earlier—Erin Kane was working there now part-time and had managed to get her the employee discount. And then she had something else in mind as well. She'd brought what she needed for it in her dance bag.

"Go change into the second outfit now," Belinda ordered. "I'll go tell the photographer you'll be ready in a few."

"As long as it's not the Flash Man," Sam joked.

"Not unless Flash had a sex-change operation recently," Belinda cracked. "Which I wouldn't put past him. Not for a minute!"

"These are some awesome pictures," Erin Kane said to Sam as she leaned over the counter at the Cheap Boutique.

"Thanks," Sam answered. "I really like them."

After she, Emma, and Carrie had finished at Super Shots—thankfully, Emma and Carrie had quit talking about Sunset Magic for the rest of the afternoon—the girls had come back to the island, their photos in hand (they'd had to wait only an hour for them to be developed), and had dropped her off at the Cheap Boutique. She'd seen a new bracelet in there a couple of days earlier that she said had her name on it.

Sam studied Erin as she looked over the photos. Erin was very pretty, with long, fabulous blond hair, and she was also overweight. Sam had had a hard time not judging her for it—for example she really believed that anyone who wanted to lose weight could, that it was just a matter of willpower.

Well, she'd been getting quite an education about that. For instance, Erin had been on just about every diet known to humanity. Now she was working on accepting herself as she was, and appreciating her own kind of beauty. It had been a revelation to Sam to find that guys were quite attracted to Erin. In fact, she was dating the Flirts' very cute, very talented new drummer, Jake Fisher.

At the moment Erin had on black leggings and an oversized black-and-white shirt with Elvis Presley's picture silkscreened on the back.

"Cool shirt," Sam told Erin.

"Oh, thanks," Erin replied. "That means a lot, coming from you. Everyone tells me you're the queen of fashion on this island."

"True," Sam agreed with a grin.

"Hey, this photo is darling!" Erin exclaimed, picking up one of Sam's shots. "Whatever inspired you to dress as a gun moll?"

Sam looked down at the photo. Her wild hair was all over the place, and she was dressed in a very oversized men's suit from the 1930s, a wide paisley tie, and black fedora on her head.

Sam laughed. "I don't know. I just thought it would be cute."

"Well, you were right," Erin commented.

"Honestly, I've never met anyone as good as you are at putting clothes together."

"It's a gift," Sam replied airily. She looked down into the glass-enclosed display counter and spied the bracelet she wanted. "Now, about that bracelet—"

Erin cut her off. "I mean it," she said.

"Well, thank you," Sam replied, eyeing the bracelet. "Now, if you could just—"

"Hey, don't you want to enter our contest?" Erin asked.

Sam knew all about the contest. A couple of weeks before, the Cheap Boutique had announced that it would hold an island-wide competition: The person who designed and sewed an outfit cool enough to be featured at the store would win five-hundred-dollars store credit and have their outfit prominently featured for sale.

"I'd love to," Sam said honestly. "But I've got a problem. I can't sew."

"At all?" Erin asked.

"I truly suck at it," Sam admitted.

"That's a drag," Erin commented, leaning down and unlocking the jewelry case.

"Yeah," Sam agreed, "because the idea

34

of a five-hundred-dollar credit to spend here is my idea of bliss." Erin laid the bracelet on the counter. As Sam took a closer look at it, she could see that it was made of cheap materials—not worth the forty-dollar price tag on it.

"You could learn," Erin offered.

"Not in the next five days," Sam replied. "That's when the contest ends, right?"

"Right," Erin said as the store manager passed the two of them on her rounds of the boutique. "So, you want the bracelet?"

"Nope," Sam declined. "I'll pass."

"Smart girl," Erin declared quietly as the store manager walked away.

"I know," Sam agreed. "Smart, gorgeous, talented, and irresistible to guys. Too bad I can't sew!"

# THREE

"Mmmmm," Sam murmured as Pres's strong fingers kneaded the muscles in the back of her neck.

"Did you say something?" Pres asked, leaning over to hear her better.

"I said mmmmm," Sam repeated, "as in 'that feels great.' You give the best back rubs in the world."

Pres laughed quietly. "I guess that means you want me to continue doing what I'm doing?"

"I love a man who can read my mind," Sam quipped, and closed her eyes to enjoy the blissful sensations Pres's fingers were creating down her spine.

Pres and Sam were at the south end of the main beach on the island. Sam had walked there from the Play Café after a quick stop at the Jacobses' house to change clothes, and the two of them had met at the big parking lot near the entrance to the beach. Pres had strapped a big picnic basket and his twelve-string acoustic guitar to the back of his motorcycle, and the two of them were now comfortably sprawled out on a beach blanket near the dunes.

It was a wonderful evening. There was a tiny sliver of moon in the sky just above the horizon, and the air temperature was still warm enough to be comfortable in a T-shirt and shorts, which was exactly what Pres was wearing. Sam, on the other hand, had picked what she thought was a perfect outfit for a date with Pres on the beach—baggy oversized cutoff jeans held up by a string of children's pop-together plastic beads, and a hot-pink bra top. For once she didn't even have on her cowboy boots—they lay beside her so that she could sink her toes into the cool sand.

The two of them had shared a wonderful cold feast of chilled lobster tails and iced cucumber slices, and were now re-laxing under the stars.

"How you doing, sweet thing?" Pres asked Sam as he leaned even farther back on the blanket to look at the night sky.

"I want you to peel me some grapes and feed them to me one at a time," Sam requested.

"Sorry, milady," Pres replied. "No grapes. Strawberries okay?"

"Can't peel strawberries," Sam said. She turned over and put her hands un-derneath her head. "Hey, sing me that song again that you sang before."

"You liked it?" Pres asked.

"I loved it," Sam answered. "We gonna do it for the band?"

"Don't think so," Pres replied, reaching for his twelve-string. "It's too country for us."

"It's awesome," Sam said. "Who'd you say wrote it?"

"Friend of mine down in Nashville," Pres answered. "A guy named Jim James. He's gonna be famous someday, I predict."

*"No,"* Sam joked. *"I'm* gonna be famous someday. But that shouldn't stop you from playing the song for me. How 'bout it, big guy?"

"How can I turn you down?" he replied, leaning over to give her a quick kiss.

Pres quickly tuned his guitar, played a hot instrumental lead-in, and then began singing in his wonderful baritone voice a song about a man who had an unstoppable desire to roam and explore the world:

> I've wandered sea to shining sea.
> It's just my struggle to be free.

He finished the tune with another instrumental riff, and the last notes carried down across the sand until they mixed with the sound of the incoming ocean waves.

"Wow," Sam said when he'd finished.

"Wish I'd written it," Pres said.

Sam looked up at the stars. "I feel just like that song sometimes, you know? Like I just want to roam the world and

40

have adventures, and never have to do what people call 'settling down.'" She pushed herself up on her elbows. "It's an awful phrase, isn't it? 'Settling down'?"

"Depends," Pres mused. "Sometimes a person finds the life he wants, and he doesn't want to roam anymore."

"That will never happen to me," Sam insisted. "I refuse!" She picked up a strawberry and popped it into her mouth. "I intend to have so many adventures that entire books will be written about me someday."

"So, what with all this roaming around," Pres asked in his easy drawl, reaching over to touch Sam's cheek tenderly, "you think you're ever gonna settle down with just one guy?"

"You think you're ever gonna settle down with just one girl?" Sam whispered back.

"Could be," Pres replied. "Who knows?" He leaned over and kissed her softly. "I never get tired of that," he murmured.

"Me, either," Sam said, and she reached for Pres and pulled him down to her for a more passionate kiss.

"I do know one thing, though," Pres said when they came up for air.

"What's that?"

"You've changed, girl," he drawled, matter-of-factly in his Tennessee accent. "Especially since your birth father came to the island. That was the biggest thing."

"You think?"

"I know," Pres stated.

Over the past two summers, Sam's entire concept of her family and where she came from had been completely rocked. First, she'd found out by accident that she was adopted. Her parents had never "gotten around" to telling her. When she finally saw her birth certificate, she learned that her birth mother was a woman in California and her birth father was an Israeli man. Sam had met her birth mother, Susan Briarly, an ex-hippie who edited children's books and lived in Oakland, near San Francisco, California.

*That was a big thing,* Sam thought as she stared up at the stars, lost in thought. *Susan told me that my father, Michael Blady, was probably dead. Then I found out this summer that not only is he alive, but that he's some kind of a hero! And then he came to visit me here on the island! That was maybe the most exciting moment of my life. Of course, I never really figured that I'd be Jewish! . . .*

"It must mean a lot to know your birth parents," Pres continued a little wistfully.

"It does," Sam said quietly. She sat up. "Do you still want to find your birth mother?" she asked, since she knew that Pres, too, was adopted.

"I still think about it," Pres admitted. "But I guess I just wasn't as lucky as you were. You found your birth mother fast."

"Yeah," she agreed. "It's still so weird to me, though."

"It helps some people," Pres commented. "Others maybe not."

"It helped me," Sam responded, reaching for another strawberry and chewing on it thoughtfully. "I feel, I don't know, just *better* about things."

"Have you heard from your birth father lately?" Pres asked.

"I got a letter from him a couple of days

43

ago," Sam answered. Michael had been writing to her regularly since they'd met.

"What did he have to say?"

"He wants me to come to Israel," Sam said, smiling into the night.

"No fooling?" Pres asked. "For a visit?"

"No," Sam joked, "forever. Of course for a visit. This fall."

"You going to go?"

"Only if you come with me, cowboy," Sam said lightly.

"Well, now—" Pres began.

"Oh, I'm only kidding," Sam assured him. "I don't expect you to traipse off to the Middle East with me. Not that I wouldn't love it."

Pres gave Sam a long look. "You really want me to come, I'm there."

"You're kidding."

"Samantha Bridges," Pres said, wrapping one arm around her shoulders, "about some things I do not kid."

She looked into his eyes. "You would really, truly, do that for me?"

Pres just smiled.

"Wow," Sam breathed. "I'm just . . . wow!"

44

Pres reached over gently and tipped Sam's face to his. Then he kissed her until she could hardly breathe. She fell back onto the sand, Pres leaning over her. He kissed her lips, her cheeks, and slowly his mouth worked his way down to her neck.

Sam reached for him, pulling him closer still, until his mouth moved back to her lips in a kiss that felt as if it would go on forever.

It practically did.

"Good morning," Sam said gaily as she came downstairs from her bedroom into the kitchen of the Jacobses' house. It was Sunday, and she didn't need to drive the twins to camp or fix their breakfasts, which had allowed her to sleep late.

"Ha!" Allie Jacobs replied from where she was sitting at the kitchen table. "I don't call eleven-thirty exactly morning."

"Yeah," her twin sister Becky added. "It's practically the afternoon."

"Got home kind of late, huh?" Allie asked. "Hot date with Pres?"

Sam didn't reply. She just grinned happily and went over to the Mr. Coffee and poured herself a cup.

"Hey, is that a hickey on your neck?" Allie asked, pointing at Sam's neck.

"My neck is not a subject for breakfast conversation," Sam replied. She blushed a little. She had tried to cover up the mark with makeup, but evidently she hadn't done a good enough job.

"Well, get down, Sam!" Becky cried. "Where else did Pres leave marks?"

"Where's your dad?" Sam asked, eager to change the subject. She stirred in a teaspoonful of sugar and some milk.

"Golfing," Allie said.

"Per usual," Becky chimed in. "What he always does on Sunday mornings. This time he went with Kiki. Gag me. He said you should stay with us until he comes home late this afternoon."

"Which is nuts," Allie added. "Like we really need you here in the middle of the day."

"I'll stay out of your way," Sam promised. "I hope he'll be back before five-thirty or so, because I've got band practice at six."

"Maybe you'll make it," Allie replied, taking a sip of orange juice.

"Hey, Sam!" a third young voice called to her as a petite girl with blond hair ambled into the kitchen. "How you doin'?"

It was Dixie Mason, one of Allie and Becky's best friends. Dixie was staying with her cousin Molly Mason for the summer. She was a counselor-in-training with the twins at Club Sunset Island.

"Hi, Dixie," Sam said. "Did you sleep over last night?"

"I did," Dixie replied. "And it was the greatest night of my life!"

"Dixie never stayed up past midnight before," Allie explained. "Can you believe it?"

"It's tough," Sam admitted. "What do your parents do back in Mississippi, keep you under lock and key?"

"Yes," Dixie answered honestly. "They're very overprotective, I guess you could say."

"So are the twins corrupting you?" Sam asked as she sat down at the table and

47

reached for the one remaining buttered bagel on the plate.

"Yes," Dixie drawled. "And it is so much fun."

"Listen, you guys," Sam said, "can you clean up down here? I've got something to do in my room."

"Call Pres to ask him why he had to be quite so obvious about his affection?" Allie guffawed. She nudged Dixie. "Check out Sam's neck!"

Sam's hand flew over her neck. "Gimme a break, okay, you guys?" She picked up her bagel and coffee. "Just please load the dishwasher, huh?"

"Can you take us shopping later?" Becky asked.

"Sure," Sam agreed. "You guys got bucks?"

"My parents sent me a check to get a new dress for church," Dixie explained.

"We thought we'd find her something see-through and short," Becky explained.

Sam was still chuckling as she padded upstairs to her room.

She finished her bagel, then reached

48

into her desk drawer for some paper and a pen.

*I'd much rather pick up the phone,* she thought to herself, *but calling Israel is definitely out of my budget. Anyway, I owe Michael a letter, and I want to do it while I'm thinking about it.*

Sam chewed gently on the end of her pen, took a big sip of coffee, and thought for a moment about what she wanted to say. Then she smiled and put the pen to the paper.

Dear Michael,

Shalom from Sunset Island! Thanks for the letter you sent me—I got it three days ago. I put up the picture you sent me of you and your parents—I'm still getting used to thinking of them as my grand-parents—on the wall near my bed.

I'll send you a brand-new one of me soon. I've got to get more copies made. I think you'll think it's funny.

The most amazing thing happened last night. You know Pres, the guy from Tennessee who is my boy-friend? Well, last night—

Just then, one of the twins—Sam couldn't tell which one—began scream-ing Sam's name as loud as she could.

"Sam! Sam! SAM! HELLLLLP!"

Sam dropped her pen and ran down the stairs. She turned the corner into the kitchen and stopped short in her tracks.

The kitchen was a foot deep in soap-suds. And the suds were pouring out of the dishwasher at a remarkable rate. It looked like a snowmaking machine at a ski area.

Meanwhile, Allie, Becky, and Dixie were running around like crazy girls, yelling Sam's name, trying to scoop up the soap-suds and dump them in the kitchen sink.

"What is happening here!" Sam cried.

"The dishwasher—"

"Turn it off!" Sam commanded. Becky scrambled over to the dishwasher and flipped the off switch.

*I can't believe not one of these girls thought to turn it off!*

"What happened?" Sam asked, surveying the layer of soap that covered the kitchen floor.

"We ran out of powdered soap for the dishwasher," Allie explained breathlessly.

"So we used the dishwashing liquid," Becky chimed in.

"We thought it would be okay," Allie added.

"It's soap, isn't it?" Becky explained.

Sam rolled her eyes. "You can't use regular dish soap in a dishwasher!"

"Y'all," Dixie said, her own eyes shining, "I have never seen anything like this in my life." And then she did a belly flop right into the thick soapsuds. Allie and Becky were right behind her. The three girls were laughing hysterically, flailing around in the soapsuds.

*Oh, what the heck, Sam thought. I'm still gonna have to get this cleaned up. I may as well have some fun first.*

She jumped right in.

# FOUR

"Wow!" Erin exclaimed when Sam walked into the living room of the Flirts' house Sunday night, "that outfit is incredible!"

"You like?" Sam asked, twirling around in a circle.

"You are so original!" Emma said. "How did you ever even come up with the idea for that?"

Sam looked down at her newest self-created outfit with satisfaction. She had on a pale blue stretchy baby's sweater that she'd found at the second-hand clothing store, Kkool Junkk. The sweater barely reached under her bustline. She held the sweater closed with two giant diaper pins to which she had glued rhinestone animals she'd found in a bin for fifty cents each. Below that she had on a long antique white cotton petticoat, to which she had attached black velvet Minnie and Mickey Mouse silhouettes. And of course she had on her red cowboy boots.

"Actually, I was watching this fashion show on TV," Sam explained, "—and I use the term 'fashion' in the loosest sense—and I saw these models wearing department store stuff that was so ordinary, it drove me crazy. I guess you could say that seeing mediocrity spurs me to greatness." Sam looked around the room. "Where are the guys?"

"In the music room," Emma replied. "They said they needed to rework the lyrics to that new song."

The guys in the band—Pres, Carrie's boyfriend Billy Sampson, the keyboard player Jay Bailey, and Jake Fisher, the new drummer who had recently been dating Erin, were putting the finishing touches on a song they had cowritten. They were planning to debut it at a benefit performance for COPE—the Citizens of Positive Ethics. COPE was a group dedicated to preserving Sunset Island's natural environment and helping the poorer citizens of the island. Kurt Ackerman, Emma's ex-boyfriend, had gotten them all involved with COPE. Kurt was the one who had shown them that beneath the wealth and glitter of the lives of the summer residents, there was a whole world of poor and suffering families who lived there year-round, most of whom eked out a meager existence as fishermen and lobstermen.

Sam looked over at Emma. *I wonder if it'll be weird for her to be performing at a benefit for COPE,* Sam thought to herself, *now that Kurt is gone. All those people she worked with in COPE were Kurt's friends. They were practically his family—after all, he grew up on this island.*

"Personally, I'd like to be in there helping them write," Erin admitted.

"So why didn't you say so?" Sam asked her.

Erin shrugged. "Well, I'm the newest member of this band. I don't want to push my way in. Do you write?"

Sam shook her head no. "I'm not even good at writing letters. Looking cute and coming up with fashion feats are my two skills in life." She put her cowboy boots up on the coffee table, which was no more than an old door resting on two piles of bricks.

"You really should enter that contest, Sam," Emma coaxed her. "I know you'd love that five-hundred-dollar credit at the Cheap Boutique!"

*Five hundred dollars' worth of clothes,* Sam thought wistfully. *There's that red leather bomber jacket I've been lusting after. And how about the black cashmere sweater with the deep V in the back? And . . .*

"I'm telling you, Sam," Erin said, breaking into Sam's thoughts, "the stuff I see you wear is more original than any of the entries that have come in so far."

"I don't suppose you're a judge?" Sam asked hopefully.

"Sorry," Erin said. "I am a mere slave of an employee. I've got no pull at all."

"Well, like I told you before," Sam said, "I don't sew. And I remember when I read the rules for the contest it said no one else could sew the garment for you, so I'm out of luck. Unless . . . one of you two is ready to give me a crash course in sewing?"

"I don't sew," Emma admitted. "I never learned."

"Gotcha!" Sam cried. "Something that Emma Cresswell does not know how to do. They should declare a national holiday or something. Miss Kane?"

"Me neither," Erin said. "It wasn't one of my priorities growing up."

"What is the world coming to?" Sam declared with despair. "Young women of America who cannot sew. What will you give up next? Cooking? Cleaning?"

"I hope so!" Erin said with a laugh.

"Anyway, I rest my case," Sam concluded. "No sewing, no entry." She reached over for a half-eaten bag of chips on the table. "Now, I wonder when the guys are gonna get done with that song. They're the ones who called this practice."

"I hope not too soon," Emma said quietly. "There's something I wanted to talk

57

over with you both. Maybe now is a good time."

Emma twisted her grandmother's pearl ring around her finger nervously. *Hmmmm,* Sam thought. *It's the COPE benefit, I'm sure. She doesn't want to do it, and she's going to tell Billy and Pres that she's not going to do the gig with the band.*

"Listen, I understand how you feel," Sam said, reaching into the bag for another handful of chips. "It's too weird for you to do this benefit because of what happened with Kurt—"

"I'm doing the benefit," Emma said. "No matter what. I'm part of the band."

"Hey, I hear Diana De Witt is going to show up, and shoot toxic waste at us with a bazooka," Erin joked. "We'd better wear decontamination suits."

They all laughed. After Diana had been kicked out of the band and Erin had been chosen as her replacement, Diana and her best friend, Lorell Courtland, had been on a single-minded campaign to be even more hateful than usual. Lately, their venom had included a series of pranks that focused on tormenting Erin about her weight.

"Diana *is* toxic waste," Sam commented, reaching into the bag for the last of the chips. "Oops. I forgot to ask you guys if you wanted any more."

"So, Emma," Erin asked, "what is it you wanted to talk to us about?"

Emma sighed. "I wanted to tell you what happened today," she said. "I've got to tell someone."

"What is it?" Sam asked.

Emma took a deep breath. "I got a letter from Kurt."

"Come on," Sam replied, looking over at the door to the music room to see if anyone was coming. No one was—she could hear Jay tinkling away on the piano. "You're hallucinating. Today's Sunday. No mail."

"Good point," Erin agreed. "But what did this hallucinatory letter say?"

"It came yesterday," Emma explained. "But Katie Hewitt got it mixed in with the stuff in her toy chest."

"So what did it say?" Sam asked again, more insistently this time.

Sam knew that just recently, Emma and Kurt had run into each other on the main beach. Kurt had come back to the island to visit his family and pick up some things to take back to Michigan, where he'd gone after he and Emma had their awful and very messy breakup.

"That's the weird part," Emma said, still nervously twisting her ring. "He just talked about what he was doing in Michigan, and that he was glad I said he could write to me, and that he might write me again."

"That's *it?*" Sam asked. "That's not gonna get you on *Oprah!*"

Emma smiled. "Maybe not," she said. "But now I don't know what to do."

"It's simple," Erin said. "You can either write him back, or not."

"So, are you upset that he didn't profess his undying love?" Sam asked.

"No," Emma replied evenly. "I didn't expect that. But . . . I don't know what I did expect! Not this friendly, chatty letter. It's like he's writing to his cousin, or something!"

"Well, maybe he's afraid to open up to

you now," Erin said. "Maybe this is his way of asking you to make a real move."

"Yeah, I agree," Sam said. She tucked her legs underneath her. "The question is, do you want to make a move? Do you want Kurt back?"

Just then Billy stuck his head through the door into the living room. "You guys ready?" he asked. "Let's get started, we're already running late."

"Gee, what timing," Erin said ruefully.

"Music doesn't wait for life," Sam quipped at Emma, heading for the music room. "So we'll get the answer later. I hope!"


"So," Sam asked Carrie expectantly, "what do you think of the unis?"

Simultaneously, she, Emma, and Erin all whirled around like models on a fashion runway.

Carrie broke into a wide grin. "Pretty cool, I'd have to say."

"Sam picked 'em," Erin said. "Or should I say, Sam put them together."

It was early Monday evening, the day after band practice, and the four girls

61

were hanging out in the backyard of Graham Perry Templeton's house. After work, Emma, Sam, and Erin had all gone shopping for new stage costumes. With Diana out of the band, and Erin being much larger than Diana, adapting the old backup singer costumes to the new trio was clearly out of the question.

"We didn't have much choice," Sam said. "We've got a gig in a couple of days."

"I think you all look great," Carrie commented. "And you'll look just as great onstage."

Finding the new costumes had been trying. The girls had gone to a few stores together, but nothing looked good or fit all of them—they were just so physically different from one another.

Emma and Erin had been ready to quit, but Sam insisted that they try Kkool Junkk, her favorite place other than the Cheap Boutique.

*That was a decision of true genius,* Sam thought to herself.

In Kkool Junkk, Sam had spotted some incredible white lace antique slips. They found slips that fit each of them, and

Sam insisted they put them on, even though she had no idea where she was going, fashion-wise. Then she spotted a table of black velvet remnants. She pulled one out and began to drape it around Emma's body, wrapping it like a toga. Then she reached into a bin of old rhinestone pins, pulled out a handful, and pinned the material together.

After that she draped a larger swathe of velvet around Erin, giving her more definition by wrapping it tighter under her bust, and then wrapping her upper arms and finally tying the material behind Erin just above her waist. Then she fastened Erin's outfit with more rhinestone pins. Finally on herself she wrapped the velvet material so that her stomach was bare, and it fell longer on one side than the other. This, too, was fastened with more rhinestone pins.

Even the salesgirls in the store had been impressed when Sam, Emma, and Erin stood in front of the full-length mirror. They were clad in three different variations on a theme, their white lace antique slips peeking out here and there from beneath the draped black velvet.

Erin grinned at Sam. "What's so cool is that you've managed to create something that flatters all three of us, I think."

"Yeah, and I did it all for about twenty dollars an outfit!" Sam added.

"I am truly impressed," Carrie said. "It's perfect! Really unique!"

Just then thirteen-year-old Ian Templeton came out into the backyard wearing Speedo swim trunks and sunglasses.

Ian was Graham and Claudia's son, and the lead singer of an industrial music band called Lord Whitehead and the Zit People—it used to be Lord Whitehead and the Zit Men, until Becky and Allie Jacobs joined the band as backup singers. Ian, of course, was Lord Whitehead.

"Hey," Ian said easily, eyeing Sam, Emma, and Erin. "Great outfits. Cool. I like the concept."

"Thanks," Sam said. She always tried to be nice to Ian, knowing how insecure he was having a father who was one of the most famous musicians on the entire planet.

"Yeah," Ian repeated, nodding seriously. "It works. I like it. Well, rock on, ladies," Ian added, and walked back into the house.

"Well," Carrie said, taking a sip of the iced tea she had brought outside with her, "if Ian approves, you know it must be right."

"You know how I crave approval from thirteen-year-old boys," Sam said, sitting on a redwood chair.

"You know," Erin said, "I have a crazy idea."

"Don't tell me," Sam said. "You're going to join the Zit People."

"Not that crazy." Erin grinned. "But I think you, Sam, should enter these costumes in the Cheap Boutique contest. You know the deadline's nine this evening—you still have time."

"How many times do I have to tell you?" Sam asked. "I didn't *sew* the costumes. So I can't enter the contest."

Erin grinned. "You're wrong," she replied.

"How so?"

"You sewed them, all right," Erin stated. "Only you didn't use any thread."

Sam's jaw hung open. "Wait, are you sure I would qualify?"

Erin nodded. "The rules don't exactly say 'sew.' They say 'construct.' 'The designer must construct the outfit herself,'" Erin quoted.

Sam stood up. "That never even occurred to me!"

"Me, neither," Erin admitted. "Not until just now, that is." She looked at her watch. "You've got exactly one hour and forty-five minutes to get one of these costumes to the Cheap Boutique and fill out an entry form."

Sam looked at Erin, then at Emma, then down at herself. "Yours," Sam decided, pointing at Emma. "Strip!"

"Here?" Emma asked, a slight grin on her face.

"You're my best friend," Sam said seriously. "I know you'd go naked for me. Oh, one other thing. I need a ride over to the Cheap Boutique."

"If I don't get arrested for driving nude

before we get there, you mean," Emma said, laughing.

Sam began to unpin Emma's dress. "Carrie, can you get Miss Modest here her clothes out of the car?"

"You got it," Carrie agreed, heading off.

"This is the coolest!" Sam exclaimed with excitement. "Five hundred big ones, here I come!"

# FIVE

"You sure put this thing together on short notice," Sam said to Emma and Carrie with admiration.

"Time is money," Carrie joked.

"Gee, that sounds like something I would say," Sam remarked as she surveyed the group of ten young teenage girls assembled on Erin Kane's back porch. The girls were chattering away with one another with excitement.

It was early the next evening. That morning, by Federal Express, a courier had delivered to Erin Kane's father several copies of the actual bottle in which Sunset Magic perfume was going to be marketed, along with three different perfume samples that he had designed.

*I've never seen Emma and Carrie spring into action like this,* Sam thought, still astonished at how quickly her friends had worked. *How they managed to put together a perfume-testing party in a day and a half is a mystery to me. But they've done it! Of course, they did get me and Erin to help them.*

On the Kanes' porch were Becky and Allie Jacobs, their best friends, Dixie Mason and Tori Lakeland, and six other girls—Sam guessed other Club Sunset Island friends of Becky and Allie's—who looked to range in age from thirteen to about seventeen. They were laughing, eating pizzas that Sam had picked up on the way to the party, listening to tapes on a portable boom box, and basically just having a blast.

Emma, Carrie, Sam, and Erin sat on four wooden rockers on the opposite side of the porch, surveying the scene. Erin's father, even though he created the perfumes that were being tested, had opted not to be around.

"Don't want to muck up the results with my male presence," he'd joked. "Just fill me in on what you guys decide, and we'll get the actual perfume produced nearly overnight."

"So," Emma said, gesturing to the younger girls, "behold, our market."

"Teens," Carrie said, and nodded.

"And incredibly cool and hip preteens," Sam added. "I started wearing perfume when I was eleven."

"You probably wore makeup at ten," Carrie teased her.

"Twelve," Sam corrected her. "Anyway, even when I was eleven, I had good taste. I didn't want to smell like my mother, and I didn't want to smell like Tinker Bell little-kid perfume, either."

"So what did you wear?" Emma wondered.

"Some stuff by an English company, I forget the name," Sam replied. "Anyway, it isn't being made anymore, so make sure this Sunset Magic stuff is something I can stand!"

Erin's mom popped her head out the back door. "Can I get you girls anything you need? More ice?"

"We're fine, thanks, Mom," Erin replied.

"I haven't seen your father this excited in years," Erin's mom confided to her daughter.

"I'm glad," Erin said sincerely.

"For my husband, fragrance is an art!" she explained. "You can't imagine how many times I've heard him rant against cheap ingredients, wasteful packaging, poor product-foisting on the public—"

"In other words, he cares," Erin translated.

"Passionately," her mother agreed.

"We're just as excited as he is," Carrie told Mrs. Kane.

"Maybe," the older woman said. "But for him it's . . . well, it's a lifelong dream to come up with his own fragrance for his own company, to see it done right, and have it be successful. And it's a dream he never thought he'd get to realize."

"We're going to do our best, Mrs. Kane," Emma promised.

"I know you will," she agreed with a smile. "Well, just let me know if you need anything."

Sam looked over at Erin. "Your parents are going to be so disappointed if this perfume thing isn't a success."

Erin shrugged. "Nothing ventured, nothing gained, right?"

"Took the words right out of my mouth," Sam said. "So, how are you planning to run the party?"

Emma reached down below her chair and picked up a couple of file folders. She opened the first folder and handed a sheet of paper to Sam.

*It's some kind of survey,* Sam realized, looking down at the document.

"Carrie and I put this together," Emma said.

"It's supposed to give us a better idea of our target market's use of fragrance," Carrie explained.

"You're filling one out, too," Emma added, handing a survey form to Sam.

"Why do you wear fragrance?" Sam read from the form. She looked at her friends. "That's simple. I wear perfume to attract guys." Sam pretended to write on her form.

"Oh, very helpful," Emma said, laughing.

Sam looked more carefully at the survey.

1.  How often do you wear fragrance? (circle one)

    daily    weekends    4–5
             only    times weekly

2.  Is there any fragrance you hate the smell of?

3.  What cosmetics do you wear regularly?

4.  This fragrance will not be packaged in a box, which means there is less waste of paper products, so it saves trees. All of its packaging will be biodegradable and it will not be tested on animals. How do you feel about this?

*How do I feel about that? I think it's great,* Sam thought to herself, answering the last question in her own mind. *There's too much packaging crap already out there, in my opinion.*

74

Sam read on. The survey was two pages long.

"Yowza," Sam commented, "this is really detailed."

"All vital information," Carrie explained.

"But do you think these kids will have the patience to fill it out?" Sam asked.

Carrie nodded. "Check it out!"

While Sam had been reading over the perfume survey, she hadn't noticed that Emma had handed out a copy of the survey to each of the girls at the party. Now they were all filling them out and Sam could see that they were taking them seriously—the loud bantering and laughter of just a few brief moments before had been replaced by total, concentrated quiet.

"I think you need to slip me five or six extra surveys," Sam joked. "I can use them to keep Becky and Allie quiet at home."

"Get to work," Carrie commanded, handing Sam a pen.

"Mom," Sam whined, "quit telling me what to do!"

"Ha-ha," Carrie said, grinning. "Just do it!"

"Okay, boss," Sam said gruffly. She took the pen and began answering the questions. By the time Sam was done, the younger girls were finished, too. They waited eagerly for someone to tell them what to do next.

"Okay," Emma said, standing up to get everyone's attention. "This is the moment you've been waiting for." She looked over at Carrie. "Well, I guess this is the moment *we've* been waiting for," she amended. "We're really excited to have you girls help us select the fragrance for Sunset Magic."

"Too cool!" Becky cried. "Sunset Island is going to have its own perfume!"

"We think it's pretty cool, too," Carrie agreed.

"So, when do we get to sniff the stuff?" Allie asked impatiently.

"Soon," Emma promised. "Today you'll be testing the three final scents. Here's another survey we'd like you to use to rate the fragrances you're about to test."

Carrie began to pass out the second survey.

"This is more writing than I do in school," Tori commented, taking one of the survey forms.

"It's for a good cause," Emma said.

Sam scanned the new form. Basically, it asked her to rate the three samples that were being tested on a scale of one to five, with the ratings as follows:

1. Yuck, makes me hurl. I totally hate it.
2. I don't like it but it doesn't actually make me gag.
3. It's okay but I wouldn't shell out any bucks for it.
4. Yeah, I like it. It's nice.
5. Wow, hoo-boy, I love it! Gimme, gimme, gimme.

"Who wrote this thing?" Sam asked with a laugh. "It's a hoot!"

"Thank you," Erin replied. "I live for humor."

Dixie Mason raised her hand, waiting for Emma to call on her.

"You don't have to raise your hand, Dixie," Emma said with a smile. "What did you want to know?"

"Well, the survey asks us to rate each perfume at first scent, then at mid-scent, then after an hour. How come?"

"Because a perfume's scent changes on your skin," Emma explained. "When you first put it on, you smell what they call the top note. Then after the perfume has been on for a while, say ten minutes or so, you smell the middle note."

"And then after the fragrance has been on for an hour or so, you smell what they call the bottom note or the dry down," Carrie added. "That's the scent that stays with you."

"And that's different on each person, depending on her body chemistry," Emma put in.

"Kinda cool, huh?" Erin asked Dixie.

Dixie nodded. "Especially the part about how the same scent can smell different on two different girls. I wonder what happens chemically to create the difference?"

"Don't mind her," Becky said. "She's a

budding genius. I care only if the perfume will attract guys!"

Carrie looked over at Sam. "What did you do, train her?"

"I do my best," Sam said modestly, then she winked at Becky.

"Uh, excuse me," Tori said. She fiddled with the rim of her Red Sox baseball cap. "Well, I don't want to be rude or anything, but . . . I don't wear perfume."

"Maybe you just never found one you like," Emma suggested.

"Maybe," Tori agreed. "But I probably never will find one I like, either. It's like makeup. It just isn't me."

"Yeah, right," Becky snorted. "Like if Pete Tilly told you he loved the smell of blueberry muffins, you wouldn't douse yourself in blueberry cologne."

"I wouldn't," Tori maintained. She gave Becky a look. "Why? Does Pete like blueberries?"

This absolutely cracked up the twins and Dixie, and Tori ended up laughing, too.

"Okay, okay," Tori finally said. "Maybe

if I found something that I just totally loved the smell of, I would wear it."

"There you go," Erin said to Carrie and Emma. "If you can win over Tori, you can win over the world!"

Emma and Carrie took out the three sample bottles, dipped numbered test strips in them, and then started to pass the test strips around. The girls took them eagerly, smelled them, and then noted their results on their surveys.

"Please don't comment out loud or make any faces as you sniff the test sticks," Carrie called out to the group. "We want to make sure you don't influence each other's ratings."

Sam took the test strips, too, starting with the one labeled MAGIC #1.

*Too sweet,* she thought. *Like something my grandmother would give me to wear when I was seven years old.*

She indicated her disapproval on the survey form, and then she took the strip labeled MAGIC #3.

*Not bad,* she thought, *but not great. Maybe a little too flowery for me. I'd wear it, but I wouldn't knock over small children to buy it.*

She then took the strip labeled MAGIC #2, feeling a little skeptical about the whole enterprise. She held it up to her nose, and took a gentle whiff.

*Whoa, baby.*

She sniffed it again. It smelled wonderful. Like the air after the rain, like the breeze at the ocean, like the way she felt when she had Pres's arms around her and they watched the sunset on the beach. . . .

*Maybe I'm fooling myself,* Sam thought. *Maybe the other two test strips have clogged up my nose.*

Sam tried to make sure her nose was clear, then she sniffed the number two test strip another time.

*I love it! It's perfect!* Sam thought with excitement. *This is the one they have to use!* For the first time she felt truly enthusiastic about Emma and Carrie's perfume enterprise as she quickly wrote the number 5, followed by five exclamation points, on her survey form after MAGIC #2.

After ten minutes, Emma and Carrie passed the testers around again. Sam liked Magic #2 even better than she had before. The group talked about everything under the sun for the next forty-five minutes—guys, love, school, parents—and then they sniffed the testers for the final time.

*I love this stuff!* Sam thought as she sniffed Magic #2 for the third time. *I only hope the teenies agree with me!*

While Emma and Carrie tallied up the surveys, the younger teens began asking Sam for fashion advice.

"What can I wear to hide my hips?" a pear-shaped girl asked Sam shyly.

"Full skirts," Sam replied confidently. "I saw this darling one at Kkool Junkk—it's covered with cowgirls on horseback—and it's cheap!"

"My parents make me wear these really conservative clothes," Dixie said. "I just don't know how to get them to let me decide what I should wear by myself!"

"Parental units have no right to dictate fashion to you beyond the age when you can actually open your mouth and pro-test," Sam decreed.

"Around age two," Becky clarified.

"So, the way I see it is—"

"We have a winner!" Carrie announced excitedly, interrupting Sam. "This is ter-rific, because there really was one over-whelming favorite!"

"Is it blueberry?" Allie called out.

"No," Carrie replied. "It's . . . can I get a drumroll, please?" she asked, look-ing over at Erin.

Erin drummed her hands on the arm of her rocking chair. "The big moment!" she cried.

"Sunset Magic is . . . number two!" Carrie revealed.

Everyone began to talk at once, with cries of "That's what I picked" and "I loved that one!"

"Hey, Carrie!" Allie cried above the noise. "When can we buy it?"

"Yo, time out," her twin sister Becky interrupted.

"What is it?" Carrie asked.

Becky stood up self-importantly. "I like this. We *all* like this. But how do we know that *guys* will like it? Did you think about *that?*"

"Who cares?" a girl with braces asked.

"We do!" Becky and Allie replied at the same time.

A rumbling went through the crowd of teenagers. Clearly, Becky's question had touched a nerve.

Emma smiled. "Actually," she said, "we have thought of that."

"So?" Becky asked. "Now what?"

"We've got a group of guys who have volunteered to do the same thing you're doing," Carrie said.

"Where are they?" Becky asked.

"We're taking the fragrances to them," Emma explained. "We didn't want you girls to be distracted."

"Oh, that's okay," Becky replied. "I don't mind being distracted. Want to spray it on me and take me over to where the guys are so they can sniff me?"

"I've raised her so well, haven't I?" Sam teased.

"If you mean does she sound just like you, the answer is yes," Emma said, laughing.

It looked like they'd found their fragrance—Sam was completely sure that the guys they were going to check with would feel the same way about Magic #2 that she did.

"Excuse me," Dixie said, "but would it be okay with ya'll if we each sprayed a little of number two on our wrists? I mean, since you said it smells different on each person and all?"

"Smart girl," Carrie commented. "Anyone who wants to be sprayed, bring me your wrist."

Most of the group eagerly lined up to be sprayed with Magic #2.

Mrs. Kane brought out some homemade cookies, which the girls gobbled up while discussing ecology, movie stars, and safe sex—in that order—and then they all sniffed Magic #2 on their own wrists.

"I love it even more now!" the girl with the braces decided. "It's like it's there but it's not too strong, you know?"

"I would definitely wear this," Becky said, sniffing her wrist again.

"Me, too," Dixie agreed.

"You want to know what's really wonderful?" Carrie asked them happily. "You guys picked the same scent that Emma and I picked as our favorite!" She turned to Tori. "Would you wear it, Tori?"

Tori sniffed her wrist again. "I don't know," she replied honestly. "I mean, it doesn't make me gag or anything. But I still don't think I'm ready for perfume."

"Don't worry," Becky assured Emma and Carrie. "Allie and I have the whole summer to work on her."

"I'll give you a detailed report on this later," Sam assured Carrie as she sprayed her own wrist with the fragrance.

"How's that?" Erin asked.

"I'm going over to see Pres later tonight," Sam explained. "I'm going to find out if this stuff really works!"

"Oh?" Erin asked innocently. "And just how can we tell if it works?"

"Because you'll have to send out a search party in the morning to find me," Sam replied nonchalantly. "And the first place I suggest you look is in Presley Travis's bodacious arms!"

# SIX

"You ready, sweet thang?" Pres drawled as he handed Sam a motorcycle helmet.

"Ready as I'll ever be," she said, strapping the helmet on.

"You know, we don't have to do this," he said. "We can just call the store and they'll be perfectly happy to tell us what happens."

"Naah," Sam said, "I'm tough. Besides, if I've won, I gotta be there for my fans."

"It's your call," Pres replied. "Let's go!" He climbed on his motorcycle, turned the key, and jumped down on the starter. The bike roared to life. Sam climbed on behind him and wrapped her arms around his waist as Pres pulled out of the Jacobses' driveway.

It was the day after the perfume-testing party, and the Cheap Boutique was about to announce the five finalists in the clothing design contest. But the boutique wasn't just posting the names of the winners. They had something special planned.

Sam had been downtown earlier that day with the twins, and had seen the display window of the Cheap Boutique had been covered over with black paper. Erin had informed Sam that behind that paper, the staff was dressing five mannequins with the five finalists' outfits— everyone would know who the five were when the window was exposed at seven-thirty P.M.

That's where Pres and Sam were heading. Sam had chosen her outfit carefully, in the event that she was one of the finalists. *No risk, no reward,* she had thought to herself, and had put together one of her more original ensembles. She was wearing men's baggy pajama bottoms bunched together at the waistline and held up by a leather belt with neon cacti painted on it. Above that she wore a T-shirt so tiny that it left her stomach bare, and over that she wore a crocheted vest that picked up the pale blue of the pajama bottoms. There was a peace symbol and a female fertility symbol on slender leather thongs draped around her neck. All in all, she was quite satisfied with her latest fashion risk.

*I tell you what,* Sam said to herself as Pres expertly maneuvered his motorcycle along the roads heading downtown. *It feels so good to be riding behind him with my arms around him and my head about two inches from his neck that I don't care if we go to the Cheap Boutique or to the tip of South America!*

It wasn't long, though, before Pres pulled the bike onto Main Street, and headed it down toward the Cheap Boutique. She felt more nervous when she saw that a crowd had already gathered outside the window—everyone knew about the contest, and had gathered to see who the finalists were.

*Too bad Emma and Carrie aren't here,* she thought to herself, holding fast to Pres's hand. *They're working. Good thing Dan gave me the night off!*

"Wow, who would have thought this would be such a big deal," Sam remarked as they approached the boutique. The staff had set up a small refreshment stand outside their main entrance, and was serving ice cold lemonade and cookies to the gathered crowd.

"It's great publicity for the store," Pres said, helping himself to a paper cup of lemonade.

Sam looked at her watch. Seven twenty-five. Her stomach did a little flip-flop. *Five minutes until I know,* she thought.

"Hey, Sam! Hey, Pres!"

Sam turned to the voice that was calling to her. It was Erin.

"Hi," Sam replied, appraising Erin from the top of her wild blond hair to the clogs on her feet. "You really look cute!"

Erin was wearing a sheer black baby doll dress over black biker shorts.

"Thanks," Erin said. "When you sell clothes at a boutique, they expect you to dress cute."

"Isn't it hard when you're such a large—" Sam stopped herself, for once conscious of the fact that what she was about to say might be insulting to Erin. "I mean," Sam amended, "did you get that outfit at the Cheap Boutique?"

"Yeah," Erin replied. "Although not much of the stuff fits me in there—which I'm sure is what you were about to say."

"Well—" Sam blushed.

"It's okay," Erin said. "Wearing a larger size is not a dirty word."

"I know," Sam agreed, trying to smile.

"I think you're looking mighty fine myself," Pres told Erin.

"Thanks," Erin said with a grin.

"So," Sam said, taking a deep breath, "did I win?"

"Can't say," Erin replied. "Too many ears around." She pointed to her boss, who was standing no more than fifteen feet away.

"Come on!" Sam wheedled in a whisper. "You're supposed to be my friend. Do you want my buddy Pres here to kick you out of the band and bring back Diana?"

"Hey, it'd be your loss," Erin said lightly. Then her boss called to her from just inside the store, and she had to turn away from Sam. "See you afterward," she promised as she hurried inside, her hair swinging behind her.

"Well, how do you like that," Sam huffed, folding her arms. "She could have told me."

"You'll find out in a second," Pres pointed out.

"She must be going inside for the unveiling," Sam said. "Well, time for my funeral. Where shall we go for the wake?"

"Hey, where's that confident girl I know and love?" Pres asked Sam, giving her a quick hug around the waist.

"I just figure some really incredible girls entered this thing," Sam said, trying to sound nonchalant. "You know, girls who learned to sew before they were weaned off their mothers' milk."

"So?" Pres asked. "You're an original."

"Yeah, probably too original," Sam muttered. "It's the story of my life."

They edged their way closer to the front window, and Sam felt more and more insecure. *Why is it that sometimes I can feel so totally confident about everything,* she wondered, *and other times I'm*

*the most insecure wuss in the world? I
don't even know why I entered this thing.*

A buzz ran through the crowd. Sam
looked at the front window. Someone was
definitely starting to pull the paper down.

Slowly the first mannequin came into
view, revealing a white shift dress with a
scoop neck and a lightning bolt of sheer
white lace set into the midriff.

"I hate to admit it, but I like that," Sam
said with a sigh. "And I could never sew
it in a zillion years."

More paper came off the window, revealing two more outfits. One featured
baggy pants covered with daisies and a
midriff-baring daisy-covered shirt. The
other was a red suit with huge black
bows instead of buttons, and smaller
bows adorning the jacket in a random
pattern.

"Second one's decent, third one sucks,"
Sam commented. "We might as well leave
now."

"Hold your horses, girl," Pres said.
"There're still two more."

More paper ripped away, revealing what
looked like a sequined prom dress in

purple and yellow with a huge bow over the bodice.

"Now, that is a true fashion disaster," Sam pronounced. "I can't believe I lost to that thing. Get me the barf bag."

"There's still one more," Pres insisted, holding tight to Sam's hand.

The last of the paper was ripped from the window. Sam shut her eyes tight, afraid to look.

"Open up," Pres told her, and she could almost hear the smile in his voice.

Slowly, she opened her eyes. And there it was—Sam's black velvet backup-singer outfit, held together with all the little second-hand rhinestone pins.

"Yes!" Sam screamed, throwing her arms around Pres with glee.

"You did it!" Pres said, giving Sam a quick hug. "I knew you could, I knew it all along."

"Five hundred dollars of clothes at the Cheap Boutique!" Sam exclaimed. "I'm already spending it in my mind!"

"Whoa, babe," Pres cautioned her. "You're a finalist, but that doesn't mean you've won the competition."

Sam scoffed. "Look at what's up there."

"Yes?"

Sam lowered her voice, realizing that the other finalists were probably in the crowd. "Well, except for the white number," she said, "there's nothing. No originality. And what is that purple and yellow thing?"

"It is kind of ugly," Pres agreed with a chuckle.

"Kind of?" Sam whispered. "The designer of that garmento should be put in prison and forced to wear her own creation! When do they announce the grand prize–winner?"

"That sign there says the day after tomorrow," Pres pointed out.

"Cool," Sam said. "Hey, there's Erin!" Erin Kane came out of the store, smiling broadly.

"Congrats, bandmate," Erin said, hugging Sam. "I wish I could have tipped you off."

"Better this way," Sam replied. "I need the anxiety."

"Where are Emma and Carrie?" Erin

asked. "I figured they'd be here to share your triumph."

"Working," Sam answered, moving closer to the door of the Cheap Boutique as the crowd started to break up.

"I should have figured," Erin said. "They were at my house just about all afternoon talking with my dad. Marketing meeting."

Sam made a face. "What a shocker," she said as if it were no big deal. But actually, she felt a little miffed. *They didn't call me to tell me they were meeting with Erin's dad,* she thought to herself.

"So, listen, I gotta go do some things for my boss," Erin explained. "I'll see you two at the gig tomorrow night."

"You got it." Pres smiled. Erin turned and went back into the store.

"Want to go for a ride?" Pres asked Sam, indicating his bike. "We can go check out the sunset."

Sam grinned but rubbed her stomach instead. "I've got a better idea."

"What's that?"

"Double-dip rum raisin at Sweet Stuff," she suggested. "Yum!"

Pres laughed. "You have no romance in your soul."

"Oh, I do," Sam assured him, "but I find it hard to be romantic when my stomach is growling."

"Okay, how about after we get you the ice cream?" Pres asked as they strolled back toward his motorcycle.

"Then," Sam said, "I will be the most romantic girl on this island."

"Lucky me," Pres said, grabbing Sam's hand and pulling her close.

"I'll say," Sam agreed.

He swatted her butt. "Don't you go getting a swelled head, now," he warned her.

She came into his arms and kissed him lightly. "I won't," she whispered.

He wrapped his arms around her waist. "I'm really happy for you, and I know how scared you were that you'd get aced out of the finals."

"Yeah," Sam admitted, "but don't spread it around, okay?"

"Your secret is safe with me," Pres assured her.

&ast; &ast; &ast;

"Mmmm," Sam said as she licked her way all around the cone. "Excellent!"

"You're down to the last dip on your triple dip," Pres pointed out.

"You can always buy me another," Sam answered jauntily.

"I can see the headline in the *Breakers*," Pres said. "CUTE GIRL EXPLODES FROM ICE CREAM OVERDOSE."

The two of them were sitting on one of the benches in the small municipal park just off Main Street, not far from the ice cream parlor. Sam had been to this park before—the island government did a really good job of keeping it full of all sorts of flowers, so the atmosphere was a mix of ocean breeze, rose, honeysuckle, and petunias.

*Could almost be a perfume,* Sam thought to herself. Then she started thinking about Carrie and Emma meeting with Mr. Kane without telling her, and an angry look crossed her face.

Pres noticed it. "What's wrong?" he asked gently.

"Oh, nothing," Sam answered lightly.

"Let me guess," Pres said quietly. "You're upset about Emma and Carrie and all the time they're spending on this Sunset Magic stuff."

Sam looked at him in astonishment. "How'd you know that?" she demanded, happy that Pres was so perceptive but a little chagrined that she herself was so easy for him to read.

"I know you," Pres said simply, reaching out to cup a passing firefly in his hands, and then opening his hand to watch the firefly blink on and off in his palm.

"I guess you do," Sam agreed, snuggling against him.

"Don't you dare get that ice cream on my jacket," Pres warned her gently.

"Have a lick," Sam offered, but he shook his head no.

"Anyway," Pres said, "it's pretty obvious. Emma and Carrie and you are best buds, and the two of them are doing this perfume thing, and you're feeling left out."

"In a way," Sam agreed reluctantly.

"In a big way," Pres said. "But from

99

what you told me, it was your choice not to be more involved, right?"

"Well—"

"Well nothing," Pres continued. "They had a business meeting today. To talk about marketing. What do you care about marketing?"

"Not much," Sam admitted, taking one last lick of her cone.

"I rest my case," Pres said.

"You don't think they still should have called me?" Sam asked.

"You can't have it both ways," Pres said. "Either you want to be involved, or you don't."

"I'm . . . what's that word that means you feel two ways at the same time?" Sam asked.

"Ambivalent," Pres filled in. "Just remember, the three of you are not joined at the hip."

"I know, but—"

"You know, sweetheart," Pres said, draping one of his arms around Sam's shoulder and holding her to him, "I think you might be feeling just a mite insecure."

"Maybe," Sam ventured.

"Well," Pres said emphatically, "from my perspective, there's one great thing about Emma and Carrie being all wrapped up in this perfume thing."

"What's that?"

"Sam Bridges has a lot more time for Presley Travis." He leaned over and kissed Sam slowly. "Mmmm, you taste sweet."

"It's the ice cream," Sam murmured, and she kissed him again. She pulled away from him and stared at him a minute. "How come you know so much about me, anyway?"

"Because I care about you," Pres said simply.

"I wonder if I know you as well as you know me," Sam mused. She cocked her head to one side. "What do you think?"

"I think you should kiss me again," Pres replied.

She playfully wagged a finger at him. "Just remember, big guy," she warned him. "You're gonna have to let me see your deep dark secrets one of these days."

"What if you don't like what you see?" Pres asked her, his eyes shining in the dark.

*Why, I think he really does feel a little insecure about that,* Sam realized. *Is it possible that deep down he's just as insecure as I am?*

"That's not possible," Sam assured him, and she sealed it with a kiss that left no room for doubt.

# SEVEN

"You ready for this?" Sam asked Emma as she fiddled with the rhinestone pins holding Emma's stage outfit together.

Emma sighed quietly. "As ready as I'll ever be, I guess."

"How about you, Erin?" Sam queried.

"Oh, I'm ready, all right," Erin replied as she tugged on her own stage costume, trying to get it to lie just right.

"Good," Sam answered.

"Ready to throw up," Erin added cheerfully.

"We are doing this voluntarily," Sam reminded her. "We wanted to be backup singers."

"Gee, that makes me feel a lot better," Erin said, managing a smile.

The girls were all in a makeshift dressing-room in the trailer behind the main stage at the COPE with the Future festival.

*Actually, it's not much more than a glorified party,* Sam thought. *COPE's charging five dollars admission, you get to throw a few cream pies at COPE members, throw paint balls at pictures of industrial magnates who are polluting the island, and listen to a few bands. Not exactly the Kansas State Fair!*

But it didn't make any difference. All three of them were nervous, anyway. It was the first time the new Flirts—with Erin instead of Diana, and Jake Fisher, the band's new drummer—were performing in public, and everybody in the band desperately wanted to be great.

A knock sounded on the door of the trailer. "Two minutes," Billy Sampson said, opening the door and sticking his head inside.

"Carrie in the crowd?" Erin asked him.

"You betcha," he replied. "Armed with a dozen cameras. Give or take ten or eleven." Then he was gone.

"It amazes me how nervous I still get before we sing," Sam said, fluffing her hair in the mirror. "I mean, we've been on tour, we've played in front of tons of people, and here I am, shaking like a leaf."

"Well," Erin said, taking a drink out of a bottle of water, "I can think of worse places to perform together for the first time."

"I can't," Emma said quietly, a scared look on her face. "Those are all Kurt's friends out there! They all hate me."

"I'll be right there with you, girlfriend," Sam said to her, squeezing her on the shoulder. Emma looked gratefully at Sam.

There was another rap at the door. It was Pres, accompanied by Jake. For just a second a face other than Jake's flashed in Sam's mind—Sly Smith—who had been their drummer from the beginning. But Sly had recently been diagnosed with AIDS, and he was home with his family in Maryland, very ill. Sam gulped hard. *Life can be so totally unfair,* she thought to herself.

Jay Bailey, the keyboard player, and

Billy came up behind Pres and Jake. Sam caught Billy's eye, and she had the feeling he was thinking about the same thing as she.

"Let's take a moment of silence for Sly," Billy suggested.

The group all joined hands, closed their eyes, and stood silently for a moment.

Billy opened his eyes and looked around at them all. "I talked to Sly yesterday," he told them. "He sent a message to everyone. He said we should go out there and kick butt!"

"Well, I think we should listen to the man," Pres said. "Let's rock and roll!"

He gave Sam a quick wink as the girls came down the trailer steps.

"Wow," Jake exclaimed, checking out Erin in her Sam-designed stage costume. "You look great!"

"Thanks," Erin replied. "Sam designed the dress."

"And God designed what's in the dress," Jake pointed out with a laugh. "Hey, maybe we should just skip the gig and—"

Erin smiled. "Don't even think of it. We've got a performance to do, buster!"

Together, they all walked toward the stage. They got to the offstage area just as the emcee was telling the crowd how happy she was to have the privilege of introducing the next act. Sam guessed there were a hundred or a hundred fifty people gathered in front of the stage.

"So put your hands together," the emcee said, "for Sunset Island's own Flirting With Danger!"

The crowd clapped politely. *Bad sign,* Sam thought, *people around here usually go wild for us.* The band raced onstage and took up their positions. Sam wondered if the lukewarm reception had anything to do with Emma and Kurt. After all, most of these people were friends of Kurt's.

Jake let fly with one of his fantastic drumrolls, and the Flirts launched into their best-known song, "Love Junkie":

You want too much
And you want too fast
You don't know nothin'

About making love last.
You're a love tornado,
That's how you get your kicks
You use me up
And move on to your next fix. . . .
You're just a Love Junkie
A Love Junkie, baby,
A Love Junkie
You're drivin' me crazy. . . .

Emma stood to Sam's left, and Erin to Sam's right, at the bank of three microphones to the left and rear of the band. "Love Junkie, baby!" the three girls sang into the mikes, wailing out the refrain in tight three-part harmony.

At the end of the chorus, the girls went into their first dance combination. *Uh-oh, here it comes,* Sam thought just as the combination was beginning. *Please, Erin, please do it right!*

Yes! Sam could see out of the corner of her eye that Erin was doing the syncopated hip-hop move and the spin exactly right. *Which just shows that you can be big and move well, I guess,* Sam mused as she did the leg crossover and came back to her mike for the next set of backup vocals.

Billy finished the song, and Jay tacked on a new ending that they had been rehearsing: rather than finishing with the customary clash of electric guitars, bass, and cymbals, the band members dropped out one by one, letting Jay cut loose a fantastic blues riff solo on his keyboard.

It was a thing of wonder. The crowd, which had been so reserved three minutes earlier, went totally nuts.

*They still love us!* Sam thought. *We won them over!*

She looked first at Emma and then at Erin. Both of them grinned back at her. Then Sam caught Carrie's eye, and actually winked as Carrie snapped off a couple of photos of the three backup singers with their arms around each other.

Pres stepped forward to his mike.

"Hey, y'all," he cried as the crowd quieted, "we're proud to be with COPE!"

"We're glad you're here!" someone in the audience cried back.

"Thank you, thank you so much," Pres

said, "that's right kind of you. We'd like to introduce the newest members of the band to you. Ladies and gentlemen, please meet Erin Kane!"

Sam saw Erin's jaw drop. Clearly, Erin wasn't expecting this. Pres turned to face Erin, an expectant look on his face.

"Go on," Sam urged her, "take a bow!" Finally Erin stepped forward and bowed, and was rewarded with a nice round of applause.

"And on drums, Jake Fisher!" Billy announced. Jake took a quick bow and did a short drumroll. The audience applauded again.

"Okay, COPE supporters," Billy yelled into his mike, "are you ready for some rock and roll?"

The crowd roared its approval back.

"This one's called 'Wild Child!'" he roared.

The band started to play, and Sam lost herself in the music.

"Whew!" Sam said, reaching for a bottle of fruit juice from the tiny refrigerator in the backstage trailer. She opened it and then drained it in one swallow. "I'm wiped out."

"Me, too," Emma said as she smiled, "but I think it went well, didn't it?"

"Awesome," Erin agreed. "Only next time you design a stage costume, Sam, take some time to think about ventilation, okay? And let's talk about wearing velvet up there in this heat!" Erin peeled part of her costume away from her left shoulder.

A knock came at the trailer door. Emma opened it. It was Carrie.

"You guys were fantastic," Carrie gushed. "So much better than with Diana."

"Thanks," Erin replied, taking a big slug of fruit juice herself. "That means a lot to me."

"Well," Carrie continued, "it's the truth." Then, without further warning, she unslung one of her cameras and started snapping pictures of her tired, sweaty friends.

"Hey," Sam protested. "No fair! My makeup's all ruined."

"Tough," Carrie grinned, "it's the real you."

There was another knock at the door. Emma, laughing at Carrie's remark, went to answer it again.

"Probably someone who wants your autograph," Erin joked as Emma approached the door.

The person knocked again. Emma opened the door—and turned white as a sheet.

Standing there was an older woman— Sam guessed about seventy-five or so, who had a mass of black hair piled up on her head and deep lines etched in her face. She was wearing a pair of weathered blue jeans and a simple blue work-shirt.

"Emma Cresswell," the woman said, a sarcastic tone in her voice. "Fancy meeting you here."

*Who is that woman?* Sam asked herself, racking her brain for the answer. *Oh, my God, I know who it is. I recognize her. It's Jade Meader, Rubie's sister. She's one of the founders of COPE. And she's really close to Kurt's family. In fact, I think that Kurt actually thinks of her as family.*

Emma attempted a smile. "Hello, Jade," she said evenly. "I hope you enjoyed the show."

"Can we speak for a moment?" Jade asked Emma, her voice sounding cold.

"Of course," Emma responded.

"Privately," Jade added, giving a significant look to Sam, Erin, and Carrie, who were watching the exchange.

Sam leaned over and squeezed Emma's hand for moral support. Emma didn't say another word. She just walked slowly out of the trailer. Jade followed her, and shut the door. As soon as they got outside, Jade started in on Emma. Sam, Erin, and Carrie could hear the whole thing through the thin walls of the trailer.

"You have a hell of a nerve," Jade said. "How dare you be up there on that stage, pretending to be a supporter of COPE!"

"I do support COPE," Emma replied.

"Young lady, after what you did to

Kurt, you are not welcome here," Jade said.

"That has nothing to do with this," Emma replied, trying to keep her voice even, but Sam could hear a tremulous quality that was totally unlike Emma.

"This is real life, young lady," Jade snapped. "This is not you in some mansion protected from the world. You hurt Kurt Ackerman, which means you hurt all of us. But I guess that's of no concern to you."

"It concerns me very much," Emma said. "But it's between Kurt and me."

"I suppose the concept of loyalty is lost on someone like you," Jade said sharply.

"That's not true—" Emma began.

"And another thing," Jade continued. "Your parents are friends of the Popes, who have a summer home on the island, right?"

"Yes, they are," Emma replied. "How is that relevant?" she added in an icy tone.

*What do the Popes have to do with this?* Sam wondered, moving closer to the wall of the trailer so she could hear better.

"I'll tell you how," Jade replied. "Your parents' friends are investors in the group that's trying to get condos built on the wetlands!"

"I'm sorry to hear that," Emma responded. "But I don't know what that has to do with me. I'm not an investor. I worked for COPE, if you remember."

"Oh, I remember," Jade said. "We have a long memory, girl, which is what you should remember."

Emma was silent for a moment. "I'm sorry about the wedding," she said quietly. "You can't know how sorry I am—"

"Well, sorry doesn't quite cut it," Jade said. "Now, here you are, leading him back on!"

"What are you talking about?" Emma asked, genuinely puzzled.

Sam peeked out the tiny window and saw Jade fold her arms and narrow her eyes at Emma. "He wrote to you."

"How did you know that?" Emma asked, shocked.

"Easy," Jade said. "Some of us actually live and work on this island, as opposed to coming here just for the summer like *some* people do. My cousin Gene is your mailman. He delivered the letter."

"I see," Emma replied, and her tone sounded like the patrician voice Emma's mother used when she was angry. "Well, I don't see that my mail delivery is any of your business."

"Kurt is my business," Jade snapped.

"Did your cousin open the letter, too?" Emma asked in a cold voice. "Because the last I heard, reading someone else's mail was a federal offense."

"Now, see here—" Jade began

Emma raised her hand. "I'm sorry. I know he didn't. But I don't think this conversation is going anywhere."

Jade stared hard at Emma. "I used to think quite a lot of you," she finally said.

"And I still think a lot of you," Emma replied. "But this is between me and Kurt. No one else."

Emma turned back to the trailer, and Sam scrambled around so as not to appear that she'd been avidly watching as well as listening to the exchange.

"You okay?" Sam asked Emma when she walked into the trailer.

"No," Emma replied honestly. She sat in the nearest chair. "Oh, Sam," she cried, "how could I have messed up my whole life?"

# EIGHT

"Are you sure you want to do this?" Carrie asked Emma, a doubtful tone in her voice.

"No," Emma admitted. "I'm not sure."

"Then let's bag this whole thing and go to the Play Café," Sam suggested. "I actually have the two of you talking about something besides that perfume, and I'd like to take advantage of it."

"Sam," Carrie said, "just chill out. Emma needs our help."

"She just said she wasn't sure," Sam reminded Carrie.

"That doesn't mean I don't want to," Emma explained quietly. "It just means . . . well, as I said, I'm not sure."

119

The three girls were upstairs at the Hewitts' house, in Emma's room, the evening after the COPE gig, which was also the night before the announcement of the Cheap Boutique contest winner.

They'd all managed to wangle a few hours off and Emma had asked Carrie and Sam to come over. She'd been badly upset by her encounter with Jade Meader, and wanted to talk with them about what to do about Kurt. She was still thinking about writing back to him, she'd told them beforehand.

So far, they'd consumed a full bowl of fruit and a basket full of potato chips, and talked about everything but Kurt—until Carrie finally brought up the subject of Emma writing back to him in response to his letter.

"The thing is," Emma said, leaning back on her bed, "I think I want to write to him, but I have no idea what to say."

"Tell him the truth," Carrie suggested. She was sitting on the bed right next to Emma.

"Tell him his body's in perfect running order but you think his personality needs a major tune-up," Sam added, reaching for some of the last potato chips. "Where's a pen? Let's get this puppy written and get out of here."

"She's so helpful," Carrie said dryly.

"Just trying to lighten things up here," Sam offered from Emma's rug as she turned onto her stomach.

"I don't know what the truth is to tell him," Emma sighed. "And I'm still so angry about what happened yesterday with Jade. She was supposed to be my friend!"

"Oh, come on," Sam countered. "You hardly knew her."

"That's not true," Emma disagreed. "We worked together on several COPE projects."

"This kind of thing always happens when a couple breaks up," Carrie said. "Everyone who was friends with them feels like they have to take sides. I have friends back home who dropped me when I broke up with Josh."

"You never told us that," Sam remarked.

"Well, it's true," Carrie said. "But you just have to move on and not let it get to you."

"Carrie's right," Sam agreed. "How many times had you actually talked to Jade before yesterday?" Sam demanded. "Three times? Four times?"

Emma thought silently for a moment. "Probably three," she said sheepishly.

"So it's not like being dissed by some major bud or something," Sam scoffed.

"She's loyal to Kurt," Carrie said. "You can't really blame her for that. He's like some kind of local hero here. And besides, she really is close to him and his family."

"Please, Jade's got her own agenda," Sam insisted. "What was it that therapist, Mrs. Miller, said to you: 'everyone's gonna have an opinion, and they're all gonna think it's their divine right to express it to you'?"

Emma sighed again. "I wish they'd just mind their own business."

"Which brings us back to what you said yesterday—that this is between you and Kurt," Sam said. She found a pen on

Emma's dresser, reached over, and handed it to Emma. "Write." She settled back down on the floor. "And wake me when you're done."

"Say what's in your heart," Carrie advised.

"Yeah," Emma agreed, but her tone was as confused as ever. "Listen, I'm just going to write something—can I read it to you when I'm done?"

"Sure," Sam and Carrie said at the same time.

"I promise I won't make fun of it, no matter what you write," Sam joked, not even bothering to open her eyes.

"That fills me with confidence," Emma replied, but she was smiling. She reached into the drawer of her nightstand and pulled out some heavily embossed stationery and began to write.

Twenty minutes passed. Sam snoozed. Carrie leafed through a magazine.

"Okay," Emma finally said. "I have something."

Carrie leaned over and kicked Sam with her foot.

"What?" Sam said, opening her eyes.

She looked over at her friends. "Drag. I was having the most luscious dream about Pres."

"Emma wrote something," Carrie informed her.

Sam turned over. "Okay, let's hear it."

"I didn't have a lot to say," Emma admitted.

"Just read it!" Sam cried. "You're driving me nuts with this!"

Emma began to read.

Dear Kurt,

Thank you for your letter. I'm glad to hear that you are fine, and doing well in Michigan—

"You sound like you're writing to a great-aunt whom you can't stand," Sam observed.

"Sam!" Carrie admonished her. "Just shut up and let Emma read!"

"Okay, okay, sorry," Sam mumbled.

"Go on," Carrie encouraged.

I find myself thinking about us a lot. I know I already told you how sorry I am that things happened the way they did. I never meant to hurt you. I know now that I wasn't ready to get married. I only wish I had known it sooner. But that doesn't mean I didn't want you, or that I wanted to be with anyone else. Can you understand that? That I was rejecting marriage and not you? I think we both made some mistakes. And now we have a choice. We can learn something from those mistakes, or we can just stay angry. Maybe writing out our thoughts to each other could be a first step. I'd like to try. No matter what you decide, I will always care about you.

Emma

Emma finished, her voice cracking with emotion again. She looked up at her friends, uncertainty clouding her eyes.

"What do you think?" she asked.

"Brave," Carrie decided, "really brave."

"You didn't sign off with 'love,'" Sam pointed out.

"Because I don't know how he'd take it," Emma admitted. She looked down at her letter. "I do love him, though," she added softly. "I can't just . . . stop loving him."

"Maybe you guys will be able to work it out," Carrie said. "It's possible."

"I don't know," Emma said with a sigh. "I wouldn't be surprised if Kurt could never really forgive me."

"Hey, let's not forget what he did to you," Sam reminded Emma, sitting up. "He pressured you, he manipulated you, he ragged on you because you're rich—"

"But look what I did to him," Emma responded.

"Yeah," Sam allowed. "But that never would have happened if he hadn't done all that other stuff to you first."

"You guys," Carrie began, "it's not a matter of who is more guilty, you know? If you still love each other, then you need to talk it all out, understand your mistakes, and handle things better in the future."

"You're sickeningly mature," Sam told her in a teasing voice.

"So . . . should I mail it?" Emma asked.

"That's up to you," Carrie replied. "But I hope you do."

"If you do, I suggest you take it on the ferry over to Portland before you mail it," Sam advised.

"Why?" Carrie asked.

"Because," Sam observed, "you never know what Cousin Gene the postman might do!"

"Ladies and gentlemen!" the owner of the Cheap Boutique, a slender, attractive woman in her forties, said into a megaphone to the big crowd of people who were gathered in front of the Cheap Boutique. "My name is Lila Cantor. I'm pleased to say it's time to announce the winner of the First Annual Cheap Boutique Island Design Contest!"

Everyone clapped, but Sam was so nervous that she bit at a fingernail instead. It was the same scene in front of the boutique as it had been a few nights before, but if anything, Sam thought, the crowd was larger. The whole gang was there: Emma, Pres, Carrie, Billy, their friends Darcy Laken and Molly Mason, who was paralyzed from the waist down and in a wheelchair. Even Dan Jacobs and the twins had come down to see if Sam was the winner.

*I hope I win I hope I win I hope I win,* Sam chanted silently to herself.

Just like the other night, the front window of the Cheap Boutique was obscured.

"Almost seven-thirty," Carrie whispered to Sam. "You nervous?"

"Naah," Sam replied. "I'm standing voluntarily in the pool of sweat forming under my feet."

"Hey, Darcy," Molly Mason said, nudging her friend, "you got any psychic flashes about this?" Darcy was known for her ESP—the only problem was that she couldn't control it, and didn't know when a premonition would hit her.

"Sorry," Darcy replied. "No luck. But I saw the outfits and I think Sam's is the best!"

The owner of the boutique started speaking again.

"It's time!" she announced. "I'm going to count down from ten to one, and when I hit one, the paper will drop off the window, and you'll see the winning outfit! Ten, nine, eight . . .

". . . four, three, two, *one!*"

The black paper seemed to magically detach from the top of the window, and flutter to the floor.

The winning outfit was revealed.

It was the white shift with the lace lightning bolt.

"Oh, well," Sam managed to say. "I guess I knew all along that I wouldn't win."

"The winning outfit," the boutique owner announced, "was created by Mr. Edgar Durning!"

A huge knot of people formed around a well-built guy with a blond ponytail who looked to Sam to be about thirty-five years old.

"A guy!" Darcy exclaimed. "Somehow I just assumed it would be a girl!"

Sam watched the winner shake hands with people as they congratulated him. *Well, if I'm going to be beaten, I might as*

*well get beat by someone older than me.
And I got to admit, it is a nice uni.*

"I hope you're not too disappointed," Erin said, coming up next to Sam.

"Win some, lose some," Sam said, trying to sound nonchalant.

"You did come in second," Erin informed her.

"Gee, great news," Sam said. "That and three bucks will get me on the ferry to Portland."

"There's more," Erin confided in a low tone.

Sam's eyebrows shot up and she waited to hear what Erin would say.

"My boss, Lila, wants to see you inside in thirty minutes," Erin said. "She asked me to tell you."

"About what?"

"Beats me," Erin said. "I'm just the messenger here."

A half hour later, Sam was sitting in Lila Cantor's tiny office in the back of the Cheap Boutique. Sam had seen Lila many times around the store—she had very short, very chic red hair, was about five foot five, and was always impeccably dressed. Now, for example, she was wearing a beige raw silk pantsuit with a double-breasted jacket over a cream-colored T-shirt. Her platform sandals were the same shade of cream as her T-shirt.

"Samantha Bridges," Lila said, putting out her hand to shake with Sam. "It's a pleasure to meet you."

"Thanks," Sam said. "You, too."

"Have a seat," Lila offered. Sam sat in the chair, and Lila perched on the edge of her desk. "I wanted you to know," Lila continued, "that I got more positive comments about your outfit from our customers than about any other of the finalists."

"Cool," Sam said, not sure where this was heading.

*If my outfit was so great,* she thought suddenly, *then why didn't I win?*

Lila smiled. "You're wondering why you didn't win, then."

"You got it," Sam admitted.

"People commented on it, yes," Lila explained. "They loved it! But not on them. They said they wouldn't buy it."

"Oh," Sam said, chagrined.

"Too original," Lila explained, picking

up a sharpened pencil and twirling it in her fingers.

Sam had to laugh. "Sorry," she said. "It's the story of my life."

"Nothing to apologize for," Lila assured her. "But, you see, my plan has always been to mass market the winning design. Mass market means a lot of people have to be willing to buy it at a reasonable price."

"I see," Sam said. "I guess the whole world isn't going to run around in my velvet creation."

"Right," Lila agreed. "Which is to your credit, I might add."

"Yeah," Sam said, "except the other guy won and I didn't."

"True," Lila said. "But maybe there is something in it for you. Actually, I'd like to offer you a job."

"Thanks," Sam said, "but I've got a job. I'm not interested in being a salesclerk."

"Not as a salesclerk," Lila said. "As a designer."

"What?"

"As a designer," Lila repeated. "For me. I'd like to make some one-of-a-kind items we could sell here. Variations on your theme in velvet. People will pay more for a one-of-a-kind, and then they're happy that it's so original."

"You're kidding," Sam said faintly.

"Hardly," Lila said, still twirling her pencil. "Whatever we sell them for, we'll pay you fifty percent. If we sell them for two hundred and fifty dollars, for example, you'll make a hundred twenty-five. Fair?"

"I guess so," Sam squeaked.

"Good," Lila said. "Bring in your first outfits later this week, okay?"

Sam's mind was racing. *Fifty percent of what they sell them for? It took me about half an hour to put those outfits together. Let's say they sell four a week at two hundred and fifty dollars. That's a thousand bucks! That means I make five hundred bucks a week!*

Sam's jaw dropped open.

For the first time in her life, she was literally speechless.

# NINE

Sam stepped into the limousine that had a vanity license plate on it which read SAMSTYLES, closed the door behind her—a hot drum solo was playing over the limo's primo sound system—and picked up the cellular phone that rested on the seat next to her. She'd gotten a message from the head buyer at Saks Fifth Avenue, the huge New York clothing store, that they'd wanted to purchase fifteen *thousand* pieces of her latest design, a velvet and lace mini shift with bell sleeves and a mandarin collar, at two hundred and fifty dollars per piece.

*Not bad,* Sam thought, *for a girl from Kansas. Not bad at all. In fact—*

"Wake up! Yo Sam! Get up!"

Sam sat up in bed, dazed.

"Wha—" she mumbled.

Allie Jacobs stuck her head in the door. "I've only been pounding on your door for the last five minutes," she said loudly. "It's eight-thirty. You've got to take us to camp today."

*Wow,* Sam thought, slowly pulling herself out of the fog of sleep and back into the real world. *What a dream! No wonder there were drums in it. Actually, I wish I were still in it. It's a lot more appealing than Allie and Becky in the morning. Hmmmm. Samstyles. I'll have to remember that.*

"What's the matter?" Sam, sitting up in bed, asked Allie.

"You gotta drive us. Here are Dad's keys, so let's go." Allie thrust the keys right at Sam's face.

"Your dad's car is here?"

"Uh-huh," Allie said. "He's sleeping."

"Whatever," Sam said foggily, taking the keys from Allie. She got up and began looking for her slippers. "I'll be down in ten minutes."

A few minutes later, Sam had dressed herself in an old Kansas State University sweatsuit, had gulped a cup of black coffee, and was behind the wheel of Dan's car, driving Becky and Allie to camp.

"So, how about if you make us some clothes," Allie suggested not two minutes after they'd pulled out of the driveway.

"What?" Sam asked, still in a fog.

"Clothes," Allie repeated. "Get with the program. Everyone knows you're gonna be designing for the Cheap Boutique."

Sam was surprised, but kept a straight face. "And how does everyone know this," she asked, "when I myself found out just last night?"

"Sam," Becky said superciliously, "you must be getting old. You've got to try to keep up."

"I am so not in the mood for this," Sam muttered.

"You know Marcus Woods from our band?" Allie asked. "Well, Lila Cantor, who owns the Cheap Boutique, is his aunt. Marcus found out from his mom, and then he called Ian last night and told him, and then Ian called me and Becky. Anyway, we were thinking maybe the Zits' backup singers could use new stage outfits."

"Hint, hint," Becky added hopefully, grinning at Sam.

"I'll think about it," Sam grinned back as she pulled into the club's parking lot. There was an old Volkswagen microbus there, from which a seemingly endless stream of kids was exiting.

"Listen," Becky said, getting out of the car, "I think it's maximum cool that you're gonna be designing clothes for the Cheap Boutique. Congrats!"

"Thanks," Sam said.

"But seriously," Becky continued, sticking her head in the car window on Sam's side, "doing costumes for the Zit People could really be your big break."

"Tomorrow," Emma said excitedly from the shallow end of one of the outdoor pools at the Sunset Country Club. "Sunset Magic will be here tomorrow morning."

"Yeah?" Sam asked, only half listening. She stretched out languidly on the bath towel she had laid on the concrete right next to the pool. She was beat. After dropping the twins off at camp, she'd spent the entire day thrift-shopping for material for her line of clothing—which she'd quickly decided she would call Sam-styles—and then hustled over to the country club. Becky and Allie were going to meet her for a ride home.

"I am so excited," Carrie said, bobbing in the water next to Emma. "I can't wait to actually see how the packaging looks."

"I thought there wasn't any packaging," Sam reminded Carrie. "You know, less waste of trees and all that good stuff."

"That's right," Carrie confirmed. "I mean the bottle design, the hang tag—do you know we even did the hang tag with soy ink so it won't pollute the environment?"

"You're a princess among women," Sam mumbled. She checked to see how much sun she was getting on her back, and thought about her plans for the rest of the day. *Home with the twins until ten-thirty tonight,* Sam thought to herself wearily, *and then I've got a date with Pres to go hang out at Surf's Up, that new club that just opened. Well, that's cool. We can't go to the Play Café every night. Meanwhile, I'm whipped!*

"So, what do you think?" Emma asked Sam.

"What?" Sam asked. "I was thinking about something else."

"I said we're getting four advance cases," Emma repeated. "I wondered if you thought that was enough."

"It sounds like a lot to me," Sam ventured to say. "But what the hell do I know?"

"You're smart," Carrie insisted. "We want your input."

"I'm too pooped to input," Sam replied. "And I've got to use my creative energy for this designing thing."

"It's incredible that you're going to be designing clothes for the Cheap Boutique," Emma told her.

Sam rose up on one elbow. "It really is,

140

isn't it?" she marveled. She searched her friends' faces. "Do you guys really think I can do this?"

"Without a doubt!" Carrie assured her. "Do you think we can pull off Sunset Magic?"

"I'd bet on it," Sam stated. She glanced at her watch to see how much more relaxation time she had before the twins arrived.

*Ten minutes. Great.*

"So, what do you do after you get these cases of perfume?" Sam asked. "I mean, do you just put it in stores, or what?"

"Mr. Kane says we need to do a big launch," Carrie explained, floating on her back.

"So we're thinking about a party," Emma said. "A launch party."

"Actually," Carrie said, "we've got a party planned. Tomorrow night at Surf's Up."

Sam sat up. "Wait a second. You're planning a party to launch Sunset Magic and you didn't even tell me about it?"

"Well, you've been really busy—" Emma began.

"Too busy for you to pick up the phone and call me? Too busy for you to even mention it?"

Carrie and Emma traded looks.

"We forgot," Carrie admitted.

Emma nodded in agreement. "I guess we got so carried away with planning everything that we forgot you didn't already know about it."

"Thanks a lot," Sam said, obviously miffed.

"Well, it's not like you've shown any real interest in the perfume," Carrie reminded Sam. "I mean, we've tried and tried to get you more involved."

"I guess," Sam reluctantly admitted, drawing her knees up to her chin. She tried to ignore her feelings of hurt. "So, you're planning this bash at that new place, Surf's Up, huh?"

Carrie nodded.

"I'm going there tonight with Pres," Sam said. "I'll give you the lowdown. How come not the Play Café?"

"We asked," Carrie said, "but they're already booked for something else. A darts tournament or something like that."

Sam was silent for a moment, staring down at her towel.

"You're mad at us," Emma guessed.

Sam shrugged. "It's no biggie."

"You're pouting," Carrie pointed out.

"No, I'm not," Sam insisted. She decided to change the subject. *I truly do not want to admit to them how left out I feel,* Sam thought to herself, *so I'm just going to drop it. After all, according to Pres, I'm supposed to be so much more mature now and everything.* "So, what are you going to do to publicize this thing?" Sam asked, trying to sound seriously mature.

"Publicize what?" two voices said from behind her at the same time. Sam turned her head to see that Becky and Allie had strolled up to her and were now deliberately blocking her sunlight. They were a few minutes early. Sam noted how cute they both looked in shorts and Club Sunset Island T-shirts.

"I'm starved," Allie said, plopping down on Sam's towel. "Can we go get a burger?"

"You eat too much," Becky told her sister. "So, what are you publicizing, your new clothing designs?"

"I'm not quite ready for that," Sam admitted.

Allie covered her eyes to shade them from the sun, and looked over at Carrie. "Don't you think it would be mondo cool if Sam designed some outfits for the Zits?"

"But Ian always performs wearing black jeans and a black T-shirt," Carrie reminded Allie.

"I know," Allie said with a sigh. "I think he's starting to look like a junior Johnny Cash or something. He needs a new look, and so do we!"

"You'll do it, won't you, Sam?" Becky begged.

"You can't afford me," Sam told her with a grin.

"But you love us," Becky reminded Sam, her eyes wide. "Well, you kind of like us, anyway. Sometimes."

"Hey, how would you guys like to come to a party tomorrow night at Surf's Up?" Carrie asked the twins.

"Really?" Becky asked with excitement. "That new place? What's the party for?"

"Sunset Magic perfume," Emma replied. "We're introducing it tomorrow night."

"Great," Becky agreed. "What should I wear?"

"Clothes," Allie told her.

"Cute or sexy?" Becky mused.

"I think you girls will have plenty of time to figure that out," Emma assured them.

Allie stood up. "Hey, maybe the Zits can record a commercial, or we can endorse your perfume, or something."

"Maybe," Emma said evenly.

*And maybe not,* Sam thought to herself with a shudder. *Talk about the kiss of death!* But then a thought flew into Sam's mind. "Hey, that's not a bad idea," Sam exclaimed. "We could get your band involved, especially Ian. And maybe Ian could get his dad to come to this party. . . ."

Carrie shot Sam a warning look.

*Okay, so she hates the idea of using Ian to get to his dad,* Sam realized, *especially because she sees people do it all the time. However, this time it's for her and Emma, so I say all bets are off!*

Allie and Becky looked at each other. "Are you saying that if I can get Ian to bring Graham to the party tomorrow, the Zits have a shot at doing a commercial for you guys?" Allie asked, her voice suspicious.

"Look, girls—" Carrie began.

"That's right," Sam interrupted.

"So, in other words," Becky said, "you're using us to get to Graham."

"Basically," Sam agreed.

"Okay, just checking," Becky said.

Allie nodded. "I can deal. We'll see what we can do. Come on, Sam."

"You're in a hurry to get home?" Sam asked, gathering up her stuff.

"Nope," Allie replied. "I'm in a hurry to get fed."

"Don't pay any attention to her," Becky advised. "We need to head right over to the Templetons. I've got to talk to Ian."

"So," Pres said to Sam as they settled together onto one of the plush velvet couches in the quieter backroom of Surf's Up, "what are you going to buy me with your first million?"

146

"Nothing," Sam replied, snuggling against her boyfriend and thoroughly enjoying the feeling of his long arm around her bare shoulders. Sam had chosen an off-the-shoulder denim blouse ruffled over the bustline, which ended about three inches above her navel. With it she wore baggy red and blue drawstring pants that settled on her hipbones, and her red cowboy boots. It was one of her more ordinary outfits.

"Nothing?" Pres queried as he reached for the Coke he'd been drinking.

"You got it," Sam replied, stifling a yawn of exhaustion. "But I think I'll buy a record company for myself. You'd like that, wouldn't you?"

"Sure," Pres bantered, "so long as it isn't Polimar!"

Sam laughed. Earlier in the summer, Diana De Witt's father had purchased Polimar Records, and Diana had used that fact to practically rip control of the Flirts away from Billy and Pres. Luckily, the transaction hadn't worked out entirely to Diana's satisfaction, and Diana was now out of the band entirely.

"Have you heard from them lately?" Sam asked.

"Actually yes," Pres replied. "Just today. Billy got a note from their A and R guy today—not Shelly Plotkin, some other guy."

"And?"

"They're still interested in us," Pres said, though he sounded dubious. "This record company stuff sure can jack you around."

"I know," Sam commiserated. She couldn't help herself—she yawned again. "But they're still interested? Really?"

Pres nodded. "But this dude goes, and I quote"—here his voice changed to corporate-speak—"'because of the corporate reorganization, it will take the company some time to restructure and pursue the signing of new bands,' end quote."

"So there's still a chance," Sam said encouragingly.

Pres took a sip of his Coke. "There's still a chance. Sometimes, though, I think the whole thing is just too big of a hassle. Not the music part," he hastened to add, "I mean this running after some corporate approval, you know?"

"Like they can tell you what music to play, and who should produce, and all that stuff, right?" Sam asked.

Pres nodded. "It won't be any different if you really get into designing, you know."

"Oh, I don't think so—"

"I'm telling you, money talks, bull walks. Whoever holds the purse strings has the power."

Sam looked at Pres hard. "I never heard you sound so cynical."

Pres shrugged and took another sip of his drink. "I've been kind of broke lately and it's getting to me." He looked around the club. "So, what do you think of this place?"

The whole place was decorated in an international surfer motif—there were posters of famous surfing champions like Nancy Emerson on the walls, surfboards hanging suspended from the ceiling, and even a miniature wave tank with a tiny beach in the middle of the room. The music, naturally, was old Beach Boys and Jan and Dean.

149

"It's okay," Sam said. "I mean, it seems kind of touristy, you know? Like they're trying too hard to be hip or something?"

"Well, there's only one Play Café," Pres said.

"Yeah," Sam agreed. She leaned over and reached for one of the coconut-battered shrimp in a basket they had ordered. "The food is good, though. In fact, the food is better than you know where."

"Oh, well," Pres said, "we never did hang there for the cuisine. Anyway, I think this is a real good place for Emma and Carrie to have their perfume launch party tomorrow."

Sam cocked her head at Pres. "Wait a second. How did you know about it?"

"They called the house and told us yesterday," Pres explained. "Why?"

*Well, I'm certainly not going to admit to him that I didn't know about it until this afternoon,* Sam thought to herself. But she felt left out all over again.

"Nothing," Sam replied. "I'm glad they got the word out so quickly, that's all."

Sam was too sleepy to even stay miffed. She yawned again, trying to hide it with her hand.

"It's not the company, is it darlin'?"

"I'm whipped," Sam admitted. "This day's been going on forever."

"You want to go?" Pres queried. "I can just finish this and drop you home."

"No way!" Sam protested. "That would mean I'll have to stand up, and it would also mean you'd have to take your arm away from my shoulder."

"You like it?" Pres asked her.

"I love it," Sam admitted, snuggling even closer.

"Then I won't move it," Pres said, and then turned his head and kissed Sam lightly on the lips. She kissed him back— fortunately, their couch was way in the rear of the backroom, and no one could see them.

*Ah,* Sam thought to herself. *This guy is world-class everything.*

She put her head down on Pres's shoulder as another wave of tiredness came over her. She closed her eyes.

*I'll only rest it here a minute,* she

thought languidly. *It just feels so comfortable and perfect. . . .*

Fifteen seconds later, she was breathing deeply. Fast asleep.

# TEN

"You fell asleep on his shoulder?!" Carrie said with a laugh the next morning. "What happened to Sam I-party-till-I-drop Bridges?"

"I guess I dropped," Sam admitted. "Anyway, I am back to my usual high-energy self today, which means I can help you guys with your perfume party."

The girls were sitting around one of the redwood tables in the Templetons' backyard, drinking iced tea and eating the grapes out of a bowl of fruit. It was the morning of the perfume launch party, and their employers, realizing how important it was to them, had all given them the day off to prepare.

*It's good we've got the day off,* Sam

153

thought, *but what's not so good is what Jeff Hewitt said to Emma!*

When Sam had arrived, Emma had reported that Jeff Hewitt, her employer, had been encouraging about the Sunset Magic launch, but had also cautioned Emma that if her business got too time-consuming, or if Emma decided to quit her job as an au pair before the end of the summer, Jeff and Jane would not be very happy about it.

"I would never do anything to hurt my relationship with Jane and Jeff," Emma had told them. "I don't know how they think I could."

"Well, you can't really blame them," Carrie had replied. "I mean, we have been spending a lot of time on this perfume thing, and you do work for them."

"I can absolutely do both," Emma had maintained.

Carrie had agreed, but Sam privately wondered how her two best friends were going to do their au pair jobs *and* the perfume *and* sing with the Flirts without something or someone suffering for it.

*Which is why they need my help with*

*this party,* Sam thought to herself. *I have enough energy for three people.*

Emma plucked another grape from the bowl. "You really want to help?" she asked Sam. "I mean, even after we—"

"Forgot to mention the party?" Sam finished for her. "I forgive you—that's just the kind of wonderful person I am."

Carrie grinned at her. "Yeah, you're okay," she allowed.

"So what's the plan for tonight?" Sam asked, pushing her sunglasses up on her head.

"What do you think of the theme Carrie and I came up with?" Emma asked, pushing a sheet of paper over to Sam to check it out.

Sam looked down and read SUNSET MAGIC—FIND THE MAGIC IN YOU! written in Emma's very neat block printing on the page.

"Not bad," she mused, "I kind of like it."

"That's not what I would call an overwhelming endorsement," Carrie remarked.

"No, it's pretty good," Sam said. "Of

course, it's not as good as *Sunset Magic—Sam's got it and she'll show you how to find it if you really suck up to her!* might be."

"I guess not, " Emma laughed.

"You're incorrigible," Carrie said.

"To know me is to love me," Sam replied, using one of her favorite expressions. "Seriously, how did you guys happen to think up your slogan? Without any help from *moi*, I might add."

"It actually had something to do with Kurt," Emma admitted. "Something he said the night we saw each other, right before he left the island again."

"Yeah?" Sam asked, intrigued.

Emma nodded. "He said I was magic," Emma said shyly, "and that started me thinking. There are so many negative messages out there—people telling you what you can't do or shouldn't do—"

"And fantasy messages," Carrie added. "You know, perfume that promises you'll become rich and famous and instantly look like a model if you just spray it on—"

"But the real magic is inside of everyone, isn't it?" Emma mused. "I felt like that was what Kurt was telling me."

"Nah," Sam decided. "He was really just telling you he still longs to get into your pants."

Carrie nudged Sam in the ribs.

"Okay, okay," Sam admitted. "I'd feel truly flattered if Pres said that about me."

"And you'd feel truly great if you could say it about yourself, right?" Carrie pointed out.

"I get your point. We've all got to believe in ourselves and all that positive self-image, self-esteem junk, right?"

"Right," Carrie agreed with a laugh.

"God, it sounds like a bad talk show," Sam groused. "So, let's talk eats for this bash. Too much serious thinking is bad for my health."

"We've got refreshments covered," Carrie said.

"What about entertainment?" Sam asked.

"Erin's going to sing," Emma reported as she took a sip of the iced tea that was sitting on the table in front of her.

"As a favor to her dad," Carrie added. "And Billy's going to do a couple of tunes."

"Hold up, hold up," Sam said. "You mean to tell me the Flirts are performing and you didn't mention that to me, either?"

"Not the Flirts," Carrie explained, "just Billy, unplugged."

"Acoustic," Sam realized. "Very cool."

"And there's one special guest," Emma reported, her eyes gleaming proudly.

"Don't tell me," Sam ordered. "Lord Whitehead and the Zit People are going to do a cover version of Graham Perry's 'Magic in a Bottle.' And they've asked you to pay them for the privilege."

"No," Carrie replied. "And I meant to tell you how much I did not appreciate your idea of using Ian and his band to get to Graham."

Sam shrugged. "Everyone else does it."

"Which is all the more reason for you not to," Carrie explained. "You know how hard it is for Ian to not be in his dad's shadow . . ."

"Yeah, I know," Sam replied, "but—"

"Hey, it doesn't matter!" Emma inter-

158

rupted softly. "Graham volunteered to do a song at the party tonight, just to help us out. There was no subterfuge or coercion involved at all!"

Sam looked at Emma. "Graham Perry *offered*? He never offers. He's practically a hermit when he's not on tour."

Emma smiled at Carrie. "I can't take any credit for it," she admitted. "I'm sure he's doing it for Carrie."

Sam shook her head. "Figures. I still can't get over the fact that you work for Graham Perry, rock superstar, and I work for Dan Jacobs, accountant."

"Well, tonight Graham Perry, superstar, is going to do something really wonderful for Carrie Alden, au pair," Carrie replied. "He's actually coming to the party, and *he's* going to sing his hit 'Magic in a Bottle' to launch our perfume!"

"How'd you pull that off?" Sam asked in amazement.

"I asked him what he thought of the idea," Carrie said.

*I have so much respect for Carrie,* Sam thought to herself. *She really is incred-*

159

*ible—she's willing to take risks. I wish I had her guts.*

Then Sam got an idea. And when she thought about it, it was Carrie having the guts to ask Graham Perry to come to the launch party that had inspired it.

*Naah,* she said to herself. *It's their party. They wouldn't be interested.*

And then another voice inside Sam said, *Well, nothing ventured, nothing gained. What do you have to lose? The worst they could say is no.*

"So," Sam said nonchalantly, "what would you think of my exhibiting a few Samstyles creations at this party? We've got the three backup-singer numbers from the Flirts, and I draped a couple more early this morning—I think maybe . . . they're pretty magical."

"It's a great idea!" Emma exclaimed.

"Oh, it's okay if you don't want me to—" Sam began.

"She just said it's a great idea," Carrie repeated, "and it is."

Sam narrowed her eyes. "Are you two sure?"

"Absolutely!" Emma insisted. "It'll give people something to look at as well as something to sniff."

Carrie sat forward quickly. "You guys, I just had a brainstorm—"

"Storm away," Sam encouraged her.

"What if . . . what if we do a mini fashion show," Carrie said with excitement. "We'll say that not only are the models wearing Sam's outfits, but they're also wearing Sunset Magic!"

"I love it!" Emma exclaimed. "I really, really love it!" She looked over at Sam. "And guess who can model?"

"Forget it," Sam protested, "I'm not modeling my own stuff. And I don't think Diana De Witt's going to be very helpful, either."

"Wrong on both guesses," Emma said with a laugh. "How about the twins! Becky and Allie would be perfect!"

"The monsters," Sam mused.

"They really have improved lately," Carrie pointed out. "You've said so yourself."

"Clearly it's due to my mature influence," Sam said regally. She thought a

161

moment. "Hand me the portable phone," she told Emma, reaching her hand out.

"You're going to call and ask them?" Carrie inquired.

"No, they're at camp," Sam reminded Carrie. "Anyway, they'd say yes even if they had to sneak out behind Dan's back. Which is exactly why I'm calling to ask Dan!"

"Here it is!" Marshall Kane said proudly as he walked through the front door of Surf's Up. "I've got it!"

"Thank goodness," Emma replied, climbing down off the chair she had been standing on. "I was afraid it wasn't going to get here on time."

"Me, too," Mr. Kane admitted, "but here it is. And it looks great!"

It was late that same afternoon. Emma, Carrie, and Sam had spent the rest of the day at Surf's Up, getting ready for the launch party. Sam had to leave periodically to prepare for her fashion show, but throughout the afternoon, a growing committee of people had stopped by to lend a hand.

162

Now, in addition to the three of them, Darcy Laken was there, and Billy and Pres, Jake Fisher, and even their friend Howie Lawrence was there to help out. Erin had wanted to come over, but she was working a shift at the Cheap Boutique. The twins had come over to the club right after camp, and were in the backroom trying on the outfits they were going to model.

Sam walked out of the back storage room, where she'd been doing fittings on Becky and Allie. "You got the stuff?" she asked gruffly in her best gangster's voice.

"Got it!" Mr. Kane assured her.

Carrie rushed over from the stage area, where she'd been adjusting a sign that read SUNSET MAGIC: FIND THE MAGIC IN YOU.

"You've got it?" she exclaimed.

Mr. Kane set down a small cardboard box on one of the cocktail tables near the door. "Right here," he said, taking out a penknife and slashing the box open. He reached inside and held up a small bottle to the light. "Well, girls, behold our brainchild."

The bottle of Sunset Magic was simple

and lovely, with nothing more compli-
cated than a hang tag on natural paper
describing the fragrance.

"I love it," Emma breathed, her eyes
shining. "It's just what I imagined."

Carrie looked at Mr. Kane and at
Emma. She couldn't keep the grin off her
face. "We did it!" she finally yelled. "We
really, really did it!"

Mr. Kane took the cap off a bottle and
sprayed a small amount on his own
wrist. He sniffed it deeply and a smile of
deep satisfaction spread across his face.
"It's wonderful," he said. He looked at
Emma and Carrie. "I don't know how to
begin to thank the two of you for this
opportunity. . . ."

"It's an opportunity for us, too," Carrie
told him.

Mr. Kane sniffed his wrist again. "It's
young and fresh and wonderful," he said.

"Well, I hope your wife doesn't wonder
whose perfume you've got on you," Sam
cracked.

Mr. Kane laughed, and Sam realized
he looked years younger than he had
when she had first met him. "I've got to

go out to my car to get the six other cases. Where do you want them?"

"In the back storage room, I guess," Carrie decided.

Mr. Kane left, pushing a dolly in front of him.

"Sam, are you gonna show us how you want us to model this stuff or not?" Becky asked, coming up to the group, Allie right behind her.

"Go practice the walk I taught you," Sam told them. "And remember to stand up straight and hold your stomachs in."

"I told you we're too fat," Becky said to her sister as the two of them headed for the small stage at the front of the restaurant.

"What am I going to do with that kid?" Sam mumbled. She looked around at the restaurant, the party decorations mostly completed. "You know, this is way cool," she said with satisfaction.

"Doesn't this seem unbelievable?" Carrie asked Sam. She sat down at the nearest table.

"It's amazing," Emma agreed. "Do you think the perfume will sell?"

Carrie shrugged. "I figure all we can do is our best, right? But one thing I know for sure, Em. I'm proud of what we've done. And . . . well, the only failure is not to try, right?"

"Right," Emma agreed. She looked down at her hands a moment, then back at Carrie and Sam. "All my life I've seen my mother just . . . expect that she'd have everything she wanted. She never really tried anything, or worked hard for anything she believed in. And I just don't want to be like that."

Carrie reached over and touched Emma's hand gently. "You're not."

"I just want you to know," Emma began, "that if and when we show any profits for Sunset Magic, I'm giving my part to charity."

Sam grinned at Emma. "Like I said, you rich Boston baroness you, it's way cool."

"Not if we don't finish decorating this place," Emma said, hustling up from the chair. "We've got a lot of work to do, and people are going to start showing up in three hours!"

The next half hour was spent in a

flurry of activity. Billy and Pres were moving furniture around and setting up sound equipment. Sam worked with the twins onstage, showing them exactly how they were supposed to model her Sam-styles. Emma and Carrie checked and double-checked the refreshment list and the guest list. There were going to be two hundred people at this party, and they wanted everything to be perfect.

"This rhinestone pin keeps coming open and digging into my shoulder," Allie complained to Sam.

"All right, all right," Sam said, "I'll fix it." She jumped up onto the tiny stage and was just beginning to undo the tiny rhinestone unicorn pin from Allie's shoulder when she heard the blast.

BOOM!

A shattering explosion rumbled through the room, and Surf's Up suddenly filled with smoke.

"What was that?" Sam screamed.

"Sam?" Becky cried fearfully.

"Take my hands," Sam yelled to the twins. "Stay right by me!" The room was getting smokier by the instant. Already

Sam could barely make out Carrie and Emma, but she managed to lead the twins over toward her friends.

"We have to get out of here!" Emma screamed.

"How?" Carrie cried.

"Follow me!" Emma screamed again, coughing and choking from the smoke-filled air. She grabbed Carrie, who grabbed Sam's hand, and Sam kept a tight grip on Becky, who held on to Allie. Suddenly Emma was overcome with smoke. She dropped Carrie's hand and doubled over, barely able to breathe.

"We have to move!" Sam insisted, groping her way through the heavy smoke. "Grab Emma!" *Please, God,* Sam prayed, *let me remember the way to the front door, because I cannot see a thing.*

Yes! Sam felt the door! The next thing she knew they were outside, each of them crying, their lungs heaving, trying to suck up fresh air.

Smoke poured from the entrance to the club. All Sam could do was to stand there, totally stupefied.

Becky and Allie grabbed for Sam's hand again. "Are you okay?" Becky asked Sam, tears running down her soot-covered face.

"I'm fine," Sam assured her. She gave Becky a hug, then she hugged Allie. "We're all fine."

In the distance they could hear the sound of fire engines from the nearby firehouse heading for the club.

"Where's Pres?" Sam asked, looking around in a panic.

"I'm here," Pres said, running up to Sam. He wrapped her in a tight embrace. "I'm here."

"Where is everyone else?" Carrie cried in a panic. "I don't think the others got out! Where's Billy?"

"I haven't seen him," Emma admitted, wiping the tears off her face.

"I have to go in after Billy!" Carrie yelled.

But just at that moment Billy, Darcy, and Howie all staggered through the front door.

"Thank God!" Carrie cried, falling into Billy's arms. "What happened?"

"I don't know," Billy said. He coughed and held Carrie close. "Is everyone okay?"

"I don't know," Sam admitted, tears still streaming down her face. "Who was in there? I was so busy with the twins, I'm not sure."

The firefighters arrived, and immediately went to work.

"Anyone still in there?" a fireman asked Emma briskly.

"I don't think so . . . oh, my God!" she screamed, frightened. "Erin's father's in there! There's a man in there! Go get him out! For God's sake, get him out!"

# ELEVEN

"We're bringing him out!" one of the fireman yelled from the door of the still-burning Surf's Up. He motioned to some of the other firefighters, who were spraying water on Surf's Up from a tangle of hoses, to clear him some room near the entrance.

*Oh, my God,* Sam thought as she huddled with her friends outside Surf's Up. *I can't believe this is happening. I can't believe this is happening.* That phrase kept repeating itself over and over in her head. *I can't believe this is happening . . .*

Time seemed to be passing in slow motion. Sam glanced over at Emma, who was sobbing hysterically, and was being comforted by Scott Phillips, a young Sunset Island police officer who they knew through Darcy Laken.

"He's alive!" the same fireman yelled.

"Thank God," Carrie cried, grabbing Sam's hand.

Sam watched, transfixed, stunned, as an ambulance backed itself up as close as the driver dared to the front of Surf's Up. Then, four firemen carried out the stretcher on which lay Mr. Kane, an oxygen mask covering his mouth and nose, and placed him the ambulance.

In seconds, the ambulance was gone, roaring away from the front of the club, its siren at maximum volume.

"Is he going to be okay?" Emma asked the firefighter.

"I couldn't say, miss," the firefighter replied honestly. He saw the horror etched across all their faces. "I think he has a good chance," he added kindly.

One of the firemen who'd helped bring Mr. Kane out of the club rushed up to the chief. He pulled off some of his protective gear and started speaking breathlessly.

"He was in the storeroom," the fireman said, sweat pouring off his smoke-blackened face. "Don't know why. The door stuck. He had passed out. Third degree burns. Smoke inhalation. Tough sucker, though, I think he's gonna make it."

"I can't believe it," Carrie said over and over again. "What happened? What happened?"

"Propane tank explosion, we're guessing," the chief of the Sunset Island fire department said. He'd arrived on the scene just minutes earlier. "That's our best guess based on what you've told us and how the flames started spreading."

"I will never forgive myself if Mr. Kane doesn't . . ." Emma began, but she couldn't even bring herself to finish the sentence.

*If Mr. Kane doesn't live,* Sam thought with horror, finishing the sentence in her own mind. *But that can't happen! It just can't!*

"Excuse me," the fire chief said, and he listened closely to information coming to him over his mobile phone unit. Then he turned back to the group who still stood there in a state of shock. "That was the medics," he explained. "Mr. Kane's condition is serious, but they've got him stabilized. He's conscious."

Carrie reached for the fire chief's arm. "That means he'll be okay?"

"It means his life is probably not in danger, although his burns are serious enough that they're medevacing him by chopper to Portland."

"Thank God," Carrie said. "Thank God."

"Somebody's got to call Erin and her mom," Sam said.

"You know his family?" the chief asked.

"They're our friends," Sam replied, choking on her tears.

"Then I suggest you call them now," the chief said. "Here. Take this cellular phone," he handed it to Sam. "You can call from my car. It'll be quieter."

"Me?" Sam asked, her face paling.

"Don't leave us," Becky begged. Both she and Allie were holding fast to Sam.

She turned to the twins. "I'll be right back," she promised. "Stay right here with Carrie and Emma."

Sam followed the fire chief to his car.

The chief had to get the Kanes' phone number from directory assistance—none of them knew it by heart, and Emma's address book, which had been in her pocketbook, was now most likely burned to a crisp inside the smoldering club.

The chief helped Sam into his car, then he politely excused himself. "I'll be right here if you need me," he assured her.

With her hand's shaking and a prayer in her heart, Sam dialed Erin's number.

"The important thing is that Mr. Kane is going to live," Carrie said as if she were trying to talk herself and everyone else into it.

It was late that same night—the night when the huge launch party for Sunset Magic was supposed to take place, but instead had turned into a horrific disaster.

As if by some unspoken signal, they'd all drifted over to the Flirts' house during the evening. Now they were all sitting in the living room: Sam, Emma, Carrie, Billy, Pres, and Jay Bailey. Some were drinking beer, some cold sodas, and no one was saying much of anything. The fire had shocked the words out of them all, more or less.

"Thank God for that," Emma agreed. She shook her head sadly. "But all that work, all that planning, all those dreams . . ." Her voice still sounded a little hoarse from all the smoke she'd inhaled.

"I'm sure ya'll can get it started again," Pres suggested.

Emma sighed. "All that perfume—gone. We're really ruined."

"I'm the one who's ruined," Sam said. "Dan Jacobs is going to kill me for putting his dear daughters in danger!"

No one laughed.

"Sorry," Sam continued. "Thought I'd inject a little levity into the proceedings. Look, at least no one is going to die."

"I know," Emma said, her voice a mixture of sadness, disappointment, and exhaustion. "But I just feel so . . ." She couldn't even finish. Tears began to stream silently down her cheeks. "I wish Kurt were here," she whispered.

The phone rang. Sam was the closest person to it, so she answered it.

"Hello?" she said, leaning back on the couch and cradling the phone under her head.

"It's Jake," the voice on the phone said to her. "Jake Fisher."

Sam knew that as soon as Jake had learned about the fire, he'd taken the ferry over to Portland to be with Erin at the Maine Medical Center.

*He must be calling us from the hospital,* Sam thought. *Where else would he be?*

Sam stuck her hand over the mouthpiece. "It's Jake," she reported. Everyone started yelling questions at her to ask Jake, and Sam had to stick her hand in the air with her palm up and motion for quiet so she could hear what Jake was saying.

"—going to need surgery," Jake was saying. "Skin grafts. There are third degree burns over twenty-five percent of his body."

"That's terrible," Sam replied.

"What?" everyone in the room asked.

Sam repeated what Jake had just told her. "How's Erin?" Sam asked him.

"Horrible," Jake reported. "But a lot better than she was a few hours ago."

"Please tell her we love her," Emma said. "And we're all praying for her dad."

"Hey," Jake said, "Mr. Kane is making jokes about it already."

"You're kidding," Sam replied.

"Nope," Jake said. "He's saying that he should never have lit that firecracker inside."

"That's amazing," Sam marveled.

"I think he's happy he's alive," Jake said. "He thinks he should have been a goner."

"If it weren't for the firemen, he would have been," Sam commented.

"He knows it, too," Jake agreed. "Look, someone else needs to use this pay phone. I'll call you guys tomorrow. Tell everyone what I told you, okay?"

"Okay," Sam said.

"And one more thing," Jake added.

"What's that?"

"He says to tell Emma and Carrie not to worry about the perfume," Jake reported. "He says that the doctors have assured him that there's nothing wrong with his nose!"

Sam hung up, and she found herself choking back her tears. It took her a moment to get a hold of herself, and then she reported what Jake had told her, word for word.

"He's an incredible man," Carrie said, wiping tears from her own eyes.

Billy rubbed his face. "I lost my best guitar, and Sam lost the clothes she designed, and you and Emma lost your perfume samples but I guess that stuff can be replaced." He hugged Carrie. "Other things are irreplaceable."

"So what do we do now?" Carrie asked.

"Pick up the pieces," Pres replied, taking a slug of his beer.

"You can do it," Billy urged her.

"I don't know," Carrie said, sounding as upset as Sam had ever heard her. "I mean, it's easy for you to say. You didn't just have your whole business ruined."

"Hey," Billy said gently, putting his hand on her knee, "it's not over. You can just get more perfume made, can't you?"

"Sure," Carrie said. "But it could take a while. They probably couldn't ship it before the end of the summer without Erin's dad to move things along."

"Carrie's right," Emma agreed. "The only reason we were able to go so quickly is because of Mr. Kane and his connections in the business."

"Well, ya'll," Pres began, "I suggest we keep some perspective here. There are people with bigger problems than us. Erin's dad, for instance."

"And the owners of Surf's Up," Jay Bailey agreed.

Carrie nodded. "I know you're right," she agreed, leaning tiredly against Billy's shoulder. "But it still hurts."

No one could disagree with her.


"But, Erin," Emma remonstrated with her friend, "I really want to help! Don't you see that the money doesn't matter to me?"

"Forget it," Erin replied, rocking gently in the chair on the back porch of her relatives' house. "Just forget it, please."

"But I don't want to forget it!" Emma insisted, her voice rising with emotion.

It was three days after the fire at Surf's Up. Erin's dad was still in the hospital—he was making a good recovery from his injuries, but Erin had just explained to Emma and Sam, who were over at her house visiting, that he still was going to have to stay in the hospital's burn unit indefinitely—several more weeks, anyway.

"My father would never accept your money," Erin said philosophically. "And that is just the way it is. So kindly back off, and let's figure out how we can get your perfume business started again."

"That's crazy," Emma said emphatically, and Sam shook her head in agreement. "He's out of work."

"He's still got partial medical insurance," Erin replied.

"I know," Emma said. "But you also told me it's just that—*partial* insurance only."

"There's some savings," Erin muttered.

"How much?" Sam asked bluntly.

"Sam!" Emma exclaimed.

"Oh, who cares about manners at a time like this?" Sam asked. "Look, I know what it's like to be broke."

"We can . . . make do," Erin said, but she didn't sound very convincing. "My mom is looking for a job—she's got a master's degree, for Pete's sake."

"In what?" Emma asked dubiously.

"Fine arts," Erin admitted.

"Not a big help wanted section for that in the *Breakers,*" Sam pointed out.

"Look, you don't know my mother," Erin said. "She'll do whatever she has to do. She applied for a job as a checkout person at the supermarket this morning. And I'm going to try to get more hours at the Cheap Boutique."

"Erin, please," Emma said, "I really want to help—"

"Emma," Erin replied, "you are a wonderful friend. This is a wonderful offer you are making. If it were up to me, I might actually say yes, as a loan. But my parents will never accept it, and that is that."

Emma sighed. "Well, if you change your mind—correction, if your parents change their minds, please let me know right away. Okay?"

"Okay," Erin replied.

Sam looked at Erin, who was staring out into the distance. *Her parents are never going to change their minds,* Sam thought. *Would I be that proud if I were suffering as bad as Erin's parents are?* Sam asked herself. And she had to be honest with herself—she really didn't know the answer.

# TWELVE

Two days later, Emma, Carrie, and Sam were spending a depressing rainy afternoon hanging out in the Templetons' house with Ian, Allie, and Becky watching Jack Nicholson's classic film *One Flew Over the Cuckoo's Nest* on video.

"Don't you think Ian looks kind of like a young Jack Nicholson?" Becky asked.

"No," Allie replied.

Becky looked at Ian and narrowed her eyes. "He does if you squint really really hard," she insisted.

Allie squinted at Ian. "Nope, still doesn't," she decided.

"So, who cares?" Ian asked. "I mean, he's old, he's totally over the hill! The

185

only real cool old guy is Jim Morrison from The Doors."

Sam shot Ian a look. "He's not old, he's dead."

"I know that," Ian said with exasperation. "But if he hadn't died, he'd be an old guy, wouldn't he? Hey, did you hear about the new song the Zits are doing about Jim Morrison? I wrote it—"

"I helped," Allie added.

"A little," Ian admitted. "I'm calling it 'Dead Poet's Society.'"

"Uh, Ian," Carrie said, "I don't think you can do that. I mean, it's the title of a movie."

Ian made a noise of disgust under his breath. "Everyone is always trying to stifle artistic freedom!"

At that moment the doorbell rang.

"I'll get it!" Ian said, untwining himself from Becky—he'd had his head in her lap and she'd had her arm around him— and rushing for the door.

"You expecting company?" Sam asked Carrie.

Carrie shook her head no. "Might be one of the other Zits," she replied. "They're known to show up whenever artistic inspiration hits them."

"I guess they need to work on their new tune, huh?" Sam asked.

Becky shot her a dirty look.

"Becky," Sam commanded, "lighten up."

"Carrie!" Ian cried out. "It's for you! Some kind of delivery!"

Sam looked quizzically at Carrie, who shrugged and got up to go to the door. Sam pushed the pause button on the remote control and switched the TV to a music video.

A few moments later, Carrie and Ian came back into the living room. Both of them were holding boxes with Federal Express markings. They set the boxes down on the floor, and Ian ran to get a pair of scissors to open them.

"What is it?" Emma asked, totally puzzled.

"I couldn't tell you," Carrie said, equally mystified. "I don't recognize the address."

Ian came back with the scissors and went to work on one of the boxes they'd brought in. Sam, Emma, and even Becky

187

and Allie gathered around to see what the mystery contents were.

Ian tore the first box open.

It was filled with bottles of Sunset Magic perfume. Perfectly packaged and ready to go.

Ian opened another box. More bottles. And another. And another.

"Looks like someone is putting you guys back in business," Sam said wryly, picking up one of the bottles and tossing it lightly in the air.

"This is unbelievable!" Carrie cried.

In the last box was an envelope with Carrie and Emma's name on the outside. Emma opened the envelope carefully, took out a one-page letter on some corporate letterhead she didn't recognize, and began to read it aloud as her friends and the kids listened, transfixed:

Dear Ms. Cresswell and Ms. Alden:

We have been informed of the unfortunate events involving Mr. Marshall Kane and the launch of your new fragrance product, Sunset Magic.

While our original agreement with Mr. Kane was to produce and ship only a limited number of samples of your new fragrance, Sunset Magic, out of respect for our long relationship with Mr. Kane, we have formulated some additional samples of your product, and send them to you herewith. Mr. Kane has told me that he encourages you to go ahead with your product launch. In fact, I believe it would mean a great deal to him. We look forward to a long and profitable association with the two of you, and wish you every success in your endeavor.

Sincerely,
Andrew Cartwright
President

"Wow," Carrie breathed.

"Double wow," Allie Jacobs echoed.

"Triple that," Becky agreed.

"Did you know that this was going to happen?" Sam asked Emma and Carrie. They both shook their heads no.

"No clue," Carrie said.

"Me neither," Emma admitted.

"Well," Sam said, "it seems to me like you're not being left with any other choice."

"What do you mean?" Carrie asked, still staring down into the boxes of fragrance.

"You're going to have to go ahead with your perfume launch," Sam replied.

"I don't know," Emma said, sitting in the nearest chair. "I don't think we can. I mean, it would be horrible to just go ahead with it when so many people are in trouble. I wish there was some way that we could help Mr. Kane, and Surf's Up, and buy—"

Sam interrupted her, leaping to her feet. She pranced around the room, saying, "I'm a genius, I'm a genius, Sam Bridges is a genius."

Everyone looked at her. "Okay," Carrie demanded, "you've thought of something. Tell us."

"Only if afterward you acknowledge the fact that I'm a genius," Sam demanded.

"You're a nutcase, I'll give you that," Ian called from across the room.

"Ignore him and talk," Carrie said.

"We can do a fund-raiser of our own!" Sam sang out, throwing her arms open wide. "Like the COPE one, but much better! We'll charge admission, and we can auction off all kinds of stuff, including Sunset Magic! We can auction some of my clothes! We'll give the money to Mr. Kane, and to Surf's Up, and to the Flirts for equipment and instruments they lost!"

Emma and Carrie stared at Sam for a moment.

"We . . . we really could," Emma said slowly.

"Hey! We can auction off a date with me!" Allie Jacobs offered.

"No one would pay anything," Becky snorted. "However, I, on the other hand, am available."

"No way!" Ian protested protectively.

"Kindly shut up," Sam told them all. Then she turned back to Emma and Carrie. "So? What do you think?"

"Sam," Carrie said, a smile lighting up her face, "you *are* a genius."

* * *

*What a scene,* Sam thought to herself as she surveyed the immense crowd. *Unbelievable. If Emma and Carrie don't make it in the perfume business, maybe they should think about becoming concert promoters.*

"There have to be five hundred people in here!" Sam exclaimed, glancing again around the Sunset Island Community Center.

"Isn't it amazing?" Emma cried, trying to be heard over the huge crowd.

"And everyone paid six bucks to get in," Sam figured. "That's . . . let's see . . . three thousand dollars already!"

It was four days later—four days that had passed in a whirlwind of activity. Once the girls had decided to do a benefit, it was like the whole thing had been meant to be—organizing it had been like dominos falling in a long, neat row.

People had started calling from all over the island—actually, from all over the Portland–Casco Bay area—to help. It turned out that Surf's Up was a locally owned business, and when word got out that the "summer people" were actually doing a benefit to help pay for the damage from the fire, it was like a floodgate of publicity opened. Everyone got behind the benefit—island residents, summer people, rich people, and poor people.

The best call of all was from a professional fund-raising firm in Portland, which volunteered its services to run the benefit party. They did fund-raising and auction parties all the time, their president had said, and it would be a pleasure to do this one for such a good cause.

In fact, the benefit, which originally had been slated for the Play Café, had to be moved to the Community Center when Emma and Carrie realized that they were selling tickets to more people than the Play Café could possibly hold.

"It's wonderful, isn't it?" Carrie asked.

"I'll tell you what's wonderful," Sam replied, "our outfits."

"Gee, could that be because you designed them?" Carrie wondered.

"Well, it could have something to do with it," Sam allowed.

The three of them were wearing variations on Sam's original draped velvet dress, only now Sam was working with different fabric. On Emma she had fashioned a white raw linen sarong, held up with red-and-pink plastic heart-shaped buttons glued to pins. Carrie wore a cotton denim dress wrapped and tucked over the bust so that it was sleeveless, with a belt made from safety pins and old pearl earrings glued to a leather belt.

And Sam had hot-pink material draped in a criss-cross over her bust, then criss-crossed again over her hips, held together by a series of old kilt pins covered with tiny seed pearls and sequins. And just this once, Sam had opted out of her red cowboy boots. Instead, she wore white platform sandals with pink flowers blooming on the toes, and little-girl white socks.

"Everyone I've talked to is so excited about the auction," Carrie yelled. Someone put a tape into the sound system they'd set up, and the sounds of Billy Joel filled the huge room.

*I'm proud of myself,* Sam thought. *Emma and Carrie put me in charge of coming up with the items to auction, and I think I outdid myself. And Lila Cantor was fine about it. She said it might even help future sales of my fashions.*

"How did you get the auction together so fast?" Carrie wondered.

"I'm a genius, remember?" Sam said with a grin.

Darcy made her way through the crowd to the trio. "Wow, you guys look hot!"

"Thanks," Carrie replied. "Sam designed all three outfits."

"I call them Samstyles," Sam explained breezily. "They are about to take over the fashion world."

Darcy looked at Emma's dress closely. "No zippers? No buttons?"

"It's all wrapped and held together with different kinds of pins," Sam explained.

"Very ingenious!" Darcy exclaimed.

"Not really!" Sam admitted with a

laugh. "I can't sew, so I had to come up with something! Anyway, soon my stuff will be for sale in the Cheap Boutique, so tell your friends and neighbors!"

"And that's not all!" Carrie said. "Later on the twins—"

But at that moment all attention was focused on the front of the room, where a stage had been set up.

"Hey, everyone, how's it going tonight?" the popular Portland deejay, Ben Burnett, called into the microphone.

The girls all turned their attention to the stage.

"We're all here tonight to benefit a very worthy cause," Burnett continued, "and I also have to say I think this is gonna be one hell of a party!"

The crowd burst into applause, and people whistled and cheered.

"It's my pleasure to introduce to you someone who doesn't need an introduction," he said, "but, hey, I'm gonna do it anyway. Ladies and gentlemen . . . Mr. Graham Perry!"

The crowd went wild.

"I can't believe he's doing this!" Emma cried happily in Sam's ear.

Graham took the stage, his acoustic guitar slung around his neck. He stood in front of the mike, which the deejay had placed in the mike stand, while the crowd continued to roar. It took forever for them to quiet down.

"Glad to be here," Graham said, leaning into the mike. "As you know, this is a benefit for three good causes—Marshall Kane, who was hurt in last week's fire, the owners of Surf's Up, and Flirting With Danger. And I'm proud to say that I personally know the girls who organized this event—Carrie Alden, Emma Cresswell, and Sam Bridges!"

The crowd gave a big round of applause, everyone looking around for Sam, Emma, and Carrie.

"Jump up here!" Darcy called, and she quickly helped the girls up onto the top of the table, where they held their hands over their heads in a victory sign while the crowd cheered.

"Thanks, ladies," Graham said. He

quickly tuned the D string on his guitar as the threesome climbed off the table.

"I wish Erin were here," Sam said to Carrie.

"Me, too," Carrie replied. She looked around at the crowd. "She'd be so proud . . . but I guess it's more important that she be with her dad in Portland right now."

"Howie's making a video," Emma pointed out, cocking her chin toward Howie Lawrence, who was taping everything. "We'll have to give Erin a copy as a present."

"Anyway," Graham continued once the crowd had quieted, "you guys know the drill. Nobody does anything for free here tonight. Right?"

"Right!" the crowd roared.

"All right!" Graham continued. "I'm taking bids now for a song of your choice. Bidding starts at fifty dollars."

"Fifty!" someone shouted out.

"A hundred!" someone else yelled.

"One twenty-five!" another person screamed.

The bidding quickly escalated to two hundred, then to three hundred dollars.

"Three hundred dollars!" Sam marveled. "Amazing."

The bidding stopped at three hundred fifty dollars. A member of the fundraising group quickly went over to the winning bidder—a well-dressed man in his forties—who smiled and gave up the money in cash.

"So?" Graham asked. "What do you want me to play?"

"'Magic in a Bottle'!" the guy yelled to Graham. "In honor of the new Sunset Magic fragrance!"

Emma turned quickly to Sam. "Wow, it's almost like we planned that!"

"We did!" Sam admitted gleefully. "That's Howie Lawrence's dad. He's a huge Graham Perry fan, and I might have begged him to request a certain song that would help promote your perfume."

Emma gave Sam a quick hug. "You are one of a kind."

"You asked for it, you got it!" Graham replied. He then launched into a haunting acoustic version of the song that had stayed at number one for three weeks a couple of years back. When he was done, the crowd went crazy.

"Thanks," Graham said when he could be heard over the crowd. "And now I'd like you to welcome a couple of friends of mine, Billy Sampson and Pres Travis!"

The bidding for a song performed by Graham, Billy, and Pres went up to three hundred dollars, too. It was purchased by Caroline and Gomez Mason, Molly's parents, who were standing near the back of the room beside Molly in her wheelchair.

"What do you want to hear?" Billy called out.

"'Let the Circle Be Unbroken,'" Molly called back.

Pres grinned. "You want to hear that old spiritual, huh?"

"I do," Molly called back.

"Let's give the lady what she wants," Graham suggested. The three musicians played the simple chords to the old church song, and sang it beautifully.

> Let the circle be unbroken
> By and by, Lord, by and by.
> There's a better world a-waiting
> In the sky, Lord, in the sky.

By the time they got to the last verse, everyone in the room was singing along, many with tears in their eyes.

"Your big moment's coming up," Carrie whispered to Sam when Pres and Billy had exited.

"How can I possibly follow that?" Sam wondered, joining in the extra round of applause for Graham, Billy, and Pres that Ben Burnett demanded.

Sam craned her neck, trying to see where the twins were. *Oh, please, girls, don't mess this up!* Sam thought to herself. *I will be humiliated for the rest of my life, and that's going to be a really really long time!*

"Ladies and gentlemen," the emcee yelled, charging up the already-hyper crowd. "We now offer you the latest rage in fashion, Samstyles!"

On cue, Becky and Allie Jacobs came strutting out from opposite sides of the stage, wearing outfits that Sam had created just for the occasion. Becky had on a wrapped black velvet miniskirt covered with hand-painted green Day-Glo peace symbols. Allie wore a shorter version of Emma's sari in red cotton with hand-painted exclamation marks dotting it. As the girls modeled, a hot song by Mariah Carey kept them on the beat.

"Hey, whaddya say!" the emcee was saying. "These outfits are the coolest!"

The audience burst into applause. Sam was beaming.

"So what am I bid for the miniskirt?" Burnett asked. "I want to hear some serious numbers!" Becky and Allie took positions near the emcee, Becky to his left, Allie to his right.

"One hundred dollars!" a young girl in the crowd yelled out.

"One fifty!" someone else called.

"Does the girl come with the skirt?" a

young man yelled, and Becky looked like she was going to die from happiness.

The bidding stopped at two hundred twenty-five dollars.

"All right!" Burnett yelled. "The finest miniskirt original ever created goes to the girl in the leather shorts in the back of the room!" Becky gave Sam a thumbs-up sign from the stage. The emcee turned to Allie. "Now, how about this fine outfit?" he asked. "Let's give it up, ladies!"

The bidding reached three hundred dollars before it stopped. The crowd cheered.

"You just raised five hundred twenty-five dollars!" Carrie yelled happily to Sam, throwing her arms around Sam.

*This is the proudest I've ever been in my life!* Sam thought, returning Carrie's hug. *I'm really making a difference here for people that I care about.*

The emcee got everyone's attention again. "Time for the last auction items of the evening," he announced.

Everyone booed.

"Now, now," he said good-naturedly,

"you're just gonna have to spend the rest of the money you've brought with you."

"I'm flat broke!" someone in the crowd yelled happily, and everyone laughed.

One of the emcee's helpers brought out a tray on which were displayed six bottles of Sunset Magic fragrance. The deejay held up one of the bottles.

"Ordinary perfume?" he asked. "I think not! It's ecologically sound, completely biodegradable, and it has no excess packaging! And Sunset Island is its test market!"

"And it smells great!" Sam yelled across the room.

"Oh, yeah, that, too," Burnett joked. "Seriously, though, it's some fine stuff, and it belongs to all of you here on the island. And best of all, it was created by Mr. Marshall Kane!"

The crowd went completely wild at this remark.

"So what am I bid for the first bottle?"

The bidding reached sixty-five dollars on the first bottle, fifty dollars on the second and third, and forty dollars on the fourth.

"How about this fifth bottle?" the emcee asked, trying to rev up the crowd again.

"Twenty dollars!" someone called out.

"Twenty-five!" said another voice.

"One thousand dollars!" said someone else.

It was Emma.

Everyone turned and looked at her. You could have heard a shoelace untie, it was so quiet.

The emcee looked nonplused. "I have a bid of one thousand dollars," he said, grinning ear to ear. "Does anyone have a higher bid?"

"Fifteen hundred dollars!" Emma shouted. A buzz went through the crowd.

*She is amazing,* Sam thought. *She's doing it to help Mr. Kane, who wouldn't take her help any other way.*

"Fifteen hundred," the emcee said, looking out at the crowd. "Do I hear—"

"Two thousand!" Emma shouted.

"Two thousand it is. Going once, going twice, sold! To the young lady with the blond hair for two thousand dollars!" the emcee said with a flourish.

"On to bottle number six!" the emcee said. "The final bottle! What am I bid?"

"A thousand!" Emma cried out.

"Five thousand!" a deep male voice boomed from the back of the room.

Everyone turned and looked to see who had bid so much. Sam almost fell off her feet.

It was Emma's father.

"Daddy," Emma breathed, tears in her eyes.

"Sold to the man in that fine double-breasted suit!" the emcee quickly yelled. "How about a final round of applause for the whole gang! Come on, let's hear it!"

As everyone applauded, Emma's father made his way over to his daughter and her friends.

"I can't believe you're here!" she cried, hugging him hard.

"You did tell me about this last night on the phone," he reminded her.

"Well, yes," Emma agreed, sounding dazed, "but I never thought . . ." She gulped hard to keep from crying. "This is the nicest thing you ever did for me."

It seemed as if the applause, the whoops and whistles, would never die down, but finally they did.

Except for one girl, standing near the front door of the community center, who just kept clapping, tears running down her face, long after everyone else had stopped.

It was Erin Kane.

# THIRTEEN

"He looks so much better," Carrie said as she, Emma, Sam, and Erin walked out of the Maine Medical Center.

It was a week after the fund-raiser. The girls had been able to give Erin's family six thousand dollars. The remaining money was used to replace the Flirts' instruments and equipment, and to help out the owner of Surf's Up.

"He really is better," Erin agreed as they walked out into the sunshine. "I think knowing that you guys have gone ahead with the perfume has helped him so much—he has something to look forward to."

"Hey, there's a park across the street,"

Sam pointed out. "Let's hang over there. Oh, I see an ice cream vendor!"

They crossed to the park and all bought ice cream cones, then they sprawled on the grass, happily licking away.

"We still have all the hard work to do," Carrie mused. "You know, trying to market the perfume."

"And then there's Samstyles," Sam put in, licking a melted drop of chocolate-chip ice cream off her hand. "I delivered the first ones to the Cheap Boutique yesterday. How soon before I'm rich and famous, that's what I want to know!"

"Too bad Darcy isn't here," Erin said with a laugh. "Maybe she'd get one of her premonitions about it."

Sam crossed her legs and looked thoughtful for a moment. "I really really really want to succeed at this," she admitted. Then she looked at her friends. "But you know, it's scary. I mean, putting yourself out there and everything."

"I feel the same way about Sunset Magic," Carrie agreed, biting into her cone.

"You?" Sam asked. "But you're always

so brave about stuff like that! Remember the time you faxed that studio and asked them to hire you to do photos of *Sunset Beach Slaughter*? And how about the time you walked right up to that photographer at the commercial shoot Emma was in in New York and got him to let you take pictures of the models!"

"That doesn't mean I'm not scared to death every time!" Carrie pointed out. "But, you know, life is short. I don't want to miss opportunities because I was too scared to go for it!"

Emma nodded. "I agree." She smiled at her friends. "Which just proves that when it comes to taking risks, I am *not* my mother's daughter!"

"I'd say you're your father's daughter," Erin said. "He's really a great guy, Emma. Imagine hopping on a plane from Boston and coming to the island to help you with the auction!"

"I'm still amazed myself," Emma admitted. She smiled again. "I never used to be close with either of my parents— Sam and Carrie know that. But . . . my dad has changed. And so have I."

Erin's face clouded over. "If anything had happened to my dad . . . I mean, if he'd been more seriously injured . . . if I'd lost him . . . well, I don't think I could have stood it."

Sam touched Erin's hand softly. "We know how you feel."

Erin looked at Sam. "Life's so weird, huh? I mean how we don't appreciate things until we almost lose them?"

"Well, I've decided to appreciate everything," Sam announced, "the Flirts, my job, Pres—"

"The monsters?" Emma teased.

"Even the monsters," Sam said. "Sometimes I really love those girls." She made a face. "God, someone get me some insulin, I'm going into sugar shock. Let me amend that. Sometimes I love 'em, and sometimes I hate 'em."

"Now, that's the real Sam," Carrie said with a laugh.

Sam hugged her knees to her chest. "The real Sam," she mused, "whoever that is." She looked at her friends. "I guess the real Sam would like to succeed at something. Something that came just from me—my brain, my talent. Something I can be proud of."

"Samstyles," Emma suggested.

Sam nodded. "But like Carrie says, even if I don't succeed, at least I'll know I tried. I won't be sitting in my rocking chair one day, with no teeth, drooling on myself, wondering about what might have been."

"Drooling on yourself?" Erin echoed, cracking up.

"Why does it have to be so scary to take chances?" Sam asked. For just a moment she sounded very young and scared.

Emma picked a wildflower from the grass and twirled it in her fingers. "I guess I could tell you the same thing that Kurt told me," Emma said softly. She tickled Sam's chin with the tiny purple flower. "Sam Bridges, you are magic. And it's okay to be scared."

"Yeah, I guess it is," Sam agreed. She smiled at Emma, then at Carrie and Erin. "And it's okay to admit it, too."

They laughed and joked around, and finally all got up and walked back to the

ice cream vendor, where they bought a
second round of cones.

And just for that moment, standing
there together in the bright afternoon
sun of a perfect summer day, they didn't
feel scared at all.

# SUNSET ISLAND MAILBOX

Dear Readers,

I can't even begin to tell you how much fun it
was to create the Sunset Magic fragrance. Teen
girls from across the country helped pick it.
Thanks to all of you who did!

How did we do it? Well, we invited readers in
various cities to tell us what they did and did not
want in a fragrance. Overwhelmingly they said it
should smell as natural as summertime, like the
ocean on Sunset Island on a moonlit night. (That
bit of poetry came from a very cool girl right here
in Nashville—thanks Sarah Sasser!)

They also said it should definitely not smell like
anything their mother or little sister would wear.
After we narrowed it down to five final scents, the
girls picked their favorite—which is what you're
sniffing right now!

In addition, they said that they did not want
wasteful, excess packaging (Save those trees!),
that they wanted the packaging to be totally biodegradable and environmentally friendly, and
most of all, that they didn't want the ingredients
to be tested on animals. Well—you asked for it, you
got it!

Hey, have you guys discovered Club Sunset
Island yet? I have to tell you, it is maximum fun to
be writing about the island from the younger
teens' point of view! The next Sunset Island book
is hot—it's called Sunset Illusions and it will be out
in August.

I've gotten some incredible casting ideas from
readers for a Sunset Island movie. Actually, a lot
of you think you should be in the movie. I do, too!
Anyway, Jeff and I are working really hard to
make the movie happen, and we'll keep you
posted.

I'd really love to get more great photos of all of
you for the wall of my office, so send 'em in! I may

be biased, but personally I think I have the cutest, coolest, most terrific readers in the world. Have a wonderful summer, and remember: The magic begins with you.

*See you on the island!*
*Best-*
Cherie Bennett

Cherie Bennett
c/o General Licensing Company
24 West 25th Street
New York, New York 10010.

*Dear Cherie,*
*I know you probably hear this all the time, but I love your books! I have read every single one of them and plan to continue doing so. Whenever I read a Sunset book, I feel as if I'm in the books, experiencing the feelings of Sam, Emma, and Carrie. I just have one question: Do you ever travel and go to bookstores and sign books for readers? If so, where? I just have to meet you!*

> *Sincerly,*
> *Courtney Yonke*
> *Kankakee, Illinois*

Dear Courtney,
   I do travel around the country to do book signings. I absolutely love meeting my readers, and I'd love to meet you, too! This spring I spoke at schools and did book signings in Tennessee, South Carolina, North Carolina, Alabama, and Florida. You'll usually find publicity in your local paper about my appearance if I'm going to be in your town. If you're ever going to be in Nashville, write

to me ahead of time and let me know! If Jeff and I are in town, we'll take you to lunch. The same invitation goes to the rest of you, too!

Best,
Cherie

*Dear Cherie,*

*I am writing in response to your request for input from readers on the positive portrayal of an overweight character in your books. I thought my story might inspire you.*

*Ever since I was a little girl, I've struggled with obesity. At times, I'll admit to being so depressed about my looks that I've considered drastic measures. But now, at almost sixteen, I've found some peace within myself.*

*I am 5'8" and weigh nearly 200 pounds. I am not a bad person nor am I unpopular. I have family, friends, and a boyfriend who is great looking and not fat. They love me because of who I am. Cherie, I think it would be a great move on your part to put an overweight character in your books. If I had had such a role model earlier on in my life maybe I wouldn't have fought so hard and long to get into size-ten jeans. It would be a great honor to think I had a small part in your decision to put a positive role model in one of your books who happens to be a size sixteen.*

*Sincerely,*
*Susan Bazzett*
*Odenton, Maryland*

Dear Susan,

It is I who am honored that you were willing to share with me and your Sunset sisters your honest and heartfelt feelings on this matter. As you know we now have the cool, gorgeous, and full-figured Erin Kane as a part of Sunset Island. I always say that beauty comes in all shapes, sizes, and colors, and anyone who is too narrow-minded to realize that needs to get over it and get a life.

Also, for all you girls out there who struggle with a weight problem, you'll be happy to know that as you get older—like college age—you'll find that there are guys who think you are wonderful and beautiful just as you are. Middle school, junior, and senior high sometimes bring out the worst in people—everyone is so desperate to fit in. There's life after high school, I promise!

Best,
Cherie

*Dear Cherie,*

*You mentioned that you want to know what readers think about Emma and Kurt getting back together. Well, I think that they messed up big time and they shouldn't be given a third or fourth chance. Adam should move there and get together with Emma because they deserve each other.*

*Also, I have a question for you. How many series do you have? I was recently at a bookstore and there seemed to be so many.*

*Love,*
*Amanda Julian*
*York, Pennsylvania*

Dear Amanda,

Thank you for your input on Emma and Kurt and Adam. I do have several series out with other publishers, but let me tell you about all the Sunset books. There's the Sunset Island series, with twenty books already in print, and many, many more to come, plus three super Specials, the Sunset After Dark trilogy, starring Darcy Laken and Molly Mason, and the all-new, incredibly cool, too exciting Club Sunset Island series, starring Allie and Becky Jacobs, and their two new best friends, Dixie Mason and Tori Lakeland. I get so many letters asking me to write faster, and as you can see I'm doing my absolute best!

Best,
Cherie

All letters become property of the publisher.